Live to Die Twice

Robert Fisher

Live to Die Twice
Copyright © 2025 Robert Fisher
ISBN: 978-1-970153-55-2
Distribution: Ingram Book Company

The main protagonists in this novel are fiction. Any similarity to persons living or dead is coincidental. Of the actual historical individuals mentioned, every effort had been made to keep their words, intentions, and actions consistent with recorded history. The endeavor was to follow chronological events as they relate to the narrative.

Cover Art by Aaron Williams

LA

Maison
La Maison Publishing
Vero Beach, Florida
The Hibiscus City
lamaisonpublishing@gmail.com

Other Books by Robert Fisher

Sanction Blue
Edge Of The Abyss
Hell To Pay
Death Dealers Incorporated
No One Lives Forever
Never Say Forever
Vengeance Is Forever

Chapter 1
The Ministry of Ungentlemanly Warfare

December Fourth, 1942, Paris, Nazi-occupied France.

The once-free streets of Paris were quiet and desolate. The city's population was under a strict curfew enforced by the occupying German military. The few Parisians that broke the curfew walked the streets under a Nazi flag. Across the street from the Gare Saint Lazare train station, three such hard-faced men sat in a B.M.W. 355. Their eyes were anxiously fixed on the train station and their watches.

In their pockets were identifications with fake names. Their real names were Hugh Barlow, Roger Talbot, and their Captain, Oliver Stapleton. All of them were former British SAS and SOE commandos recruited into the most secretive branch of MI6 codenamed Equinox. Each of them was a veteran of previous operations against the Nazis. They were dressed in standard civilian clothes, chosen specifically so they would not look like tourists but instead like regular Parisians.

While Barlow and Talbot carried a Browning Hi-Power under their jackets, Stapleton carried an Enfield No. 2 Mark 1 revolver under his. They had been preparing for this mission for weeks, and tonight was the night when they would soon find out if their training would pay off. As Barlow and Talbot watched the building, Stapleton checked his wristwatch. It read five minutes past midnight.

"Ready, Sir?" asked Barlow.

"Yes, it's time. You all have your objectives. Remember, these blighters aren't your average Jerry goons. They're Aquarius, bloody the cream of the crop," said Stapleton.

"More like the worst of the worst," muttered Talbot.

"Call them whatever you want, Sir. They're the same old Jerry bastards," said Barlow.

"Regardless, let's go over the plan again," said Stapleton, Barlow, and Talbot, moaning, slightly annoyed.

"The package should be there by now. We will go in, get it, and drive out to the country where there's a plane waiting to fly us back to England," said Stapleton. "The package is in a crate marked SPEERSPITZE, except mostly MP-40s and pistols. The bastards have shut down the station, so there should be no civilians."

"Ready, gents?" asked Stapleton. The men nodded and pulled out their pistols, cocked them and holstered them. "Right then, let's get on with it."

The three men got out of the car and walked casually into the train station. The train station was empty and quiet except for the echoes of orders being barked in German and crates being moved in the back. Each of them walked with their hands in their pockets across the lobby to the train platforms in the back.

"Halt!!" yelled a loud, angry voice in a thick Bavarian accent.

They looked over and saw a German soldier walking towards them. As he approached them, he unslung his weapon, a Schmiesser MP-40 submachine gun, and aimed it at them.

The three men looked at Stapleton; he nodded, and they nodded back at him, ignoring the guard's requests. Barlow pulled out his Browning and fired two shots at the man's forehead. Before the soldier's body hit the floor, the others drew their pistols. Stapleton snapped his fingers and pointed to the dead soldier's gun. Barlow nodded and ran over to it, picking it up as well as some ammunition.

Suddenly, drawn by the gunfire, two more guards ran into the lobby, submachine guns drawn. Talbot and Stapleton turned and shot them as they ran into the lobby. They ran over to them and picked up their submachine guns.

"Time for the main event, lads," muttered Barlow as they cocked the machine guns. They ran across the lobby and onto the train platforms. Upon entering the platforms of the station, they were greeted not by the grayish-green of the Wehrmacht but by the ebon-clad agents of Aquarius.

"Compliments of the queen, Jerries!" yelled Barlow as he opened fire on them before the guards could respond. Talbot and Stapleton jumped for cover behind a wall as they fired at them. The soldiers scrambled to return fire as Barlow ran behind several crates. Talbot and Stapleton jumped up and fired several short bursts of fire at the guards. They ducked back behind the cover as the remaining soldiers returned fire. As they reloaded, Talbot noticed a crate marked SPEERSPITZE on one of the platforms.

"Sir, it's the crate!" yelled Talbot, pointing to it.

"Go get it, we'll cover you," barked Stapleton over the staccato of gunfire.

Talbot nodded and ran towards the crate while Stapleton and Barlow fired at the attacking Nazis, drawing their fire away from him. Talbot smashed it open with the butt of the gun and saw inside surrounded by hay with a small metal box the size of his arm.

"Talbot! Behind you!" yelled Barlow as a German soldier approached him from behind.

Talbot swung around, grabbed him by his collar, and kicked him in the stomach, then grabbed him by his neck and shoved him into one of the trains. He quickly grabbed the box and looked over at Stapleton and Barlow.

"Got it!" yelled Stapleton.

"Then let's get the bloody hell out of here," barked Barlow.

As Talbot ran to the lobby, Stapleton and Barlow covered him. Once he was there, Stapleton pulled a small grenade out of his pocket and scanned the room until he saw a crate marked Ammo in German.

He pulled the pin and threw the grenade at the crate. "Last call, Gents!" yelled Stapleton.

The two men ran across the lobby just as the grenade exploded in a thunderous fireball. As they exited the train station, Talbot drove up to them in the car. The three men got in and drove off into the night as fast as they could, as smoke from the fire wafted up into the cool Parisian night.

Chapter 2
The Call to Adventure

Present Day, Agattu Island, Alaska, USA

The Near Island chain is the smallest and farthest western part of the Aleutian Islands. Agattu is one of the largest uninhabited islands in the chain. At least it was until six months ago, there was a shack on its shore. The shack belonged to the island's only inhabitant, a man named Simon Dio Kane. A former SEAL Team Six operator and agent of the CIA's black ops division codenamed Silhouette, Simon lived a quiet and lonely life on the island, hunting and fishing.

He rarely thought about the circumstances that had brought him to this isolated existence so far from civilization. Though, he did occasionally think about what happened to his friends, especially Mai Yunao. His tranquil existence was interrupted only by the occasional nightmare. Usually, they were about the loss of his wife and the events of the previous year. He woke up in his bed and looked at his watch, annoyed that he had overslept.

He got up and walked over to the mirror he had purchased, along with his new clothes, furniture, and sleeping bag, in Zarubino. His once clean-shaven face was now overgrown with a long black beard; his formerly short, slicked black hair was now long and filthy. Staring back at him was the black eye patch over his right eye. The eye patch and the contents of the chest next to his sleeping bag were all that reminded him of his old life. Across from his bed was a table with his clothes on it. His wardrobe consisted of a brown sweater with a Soviet-era naval coat, black boots, black pants, and a black stocking cap.

He often wondered what his old friends would think if they saw him now. He shrugged, dismissing the idea, and quickly got dressed. He walked outside, ready for another day of fishing and hunting. To his surprise, there was an inflatable boat next to the wooden rowboat he used for fishing.

"Seriously, bro, six months and you go full ZZ Top?" said a familiar voice from behind him.

Simon recognized the voice instantly and turned around to see an old friend of his from his time in Silhouette leaning against his shack. "What the hell are you doing here?"

"Nice to see you too," said Deon sarcastically. "So, how's the castaway lifestyle treating you?"

"I'm getting by," replied Simon. He noticed Deon was wearing the same clothes he had on the last time Simon saw him, in addition to a dark, light brown jacket with a fur lining.

Deon wore a yellow t-shirt; across his chest was the strap of his leather shoulder holster with black pants and short hair. He was a tall, muscular black man as tall as Simon. Deon glanced to his left and right, then back at Simon.

"I can see that," said Mack drily.

"Again, what do you want?" asked Simon, annoyed at not getting an answer.

Deon patiently removed his glasses and put them in his pocket. "I want to make you an offer."

"No," said Simon bluntly.

"You didn't even hear it yet," protested Deon.

"Doesn't matter, the answer's no," grunted Simon as he turned toward his boat.

"At least hear me out first," said Deon as he placed his hand on Simon's shoulder. "We've known each other too long."

Simon shrugged and looked out to sea. In the distance, he could see a small seaplane bobbing in the waves. He looked back at Deon, "The others are here with you now, aren't they?

"Yep, except for Dennis, he's still on Sankan," answered Deon.

"Come inside," said Simon as he walked into the shack. He followed Simon into the shack. Simon leaned against the wall while Deon sat in a chair next to the table.

"Nice place," grunted Deon sarcastically.

"Better than that dump of yours in Frisco," replied Simon drily.

Deon grimaced. "Only tourists call it Frisco."

"So you were saying," said Simon as he crossed his arms, implying that he wanted Deon to get to the point of his visit.

"After what happened in North Korea, Mack, Dennis, Siobhan, and me decided to form a team and become soldiers for hire," began Deon.

"You sound like mercenaries," grunted Simon.

"Yes, but the difference is we go after the bad guys. The good guys can't or won't from our HQ on Sankan Island," Deon answered.

"Like the A-team?" replied Simon.

"Exactly," answered Deon as he snapped his fingers. "After we saved his daughter, the Triad helped us get set up and everything…even have our own HQ."

"On Sankan Island?" asked Simon.

"I know the place is a shithole, but it's a perfect HQ for us since the Triad, the Syndicate, and the Guild all have a presence there that we can use to our advantage," replied Deon.

"Good point. It also helps that no country claims it, so you won't get hassled by police. Whose idea was it?" Simon asked.

Mack's. The idea came to him after seeing how well we worked together in Iceland and North Korea," continued Deon.

"So, where do I come in?" Simon asked as if he hadn't already figured it out.

"It occurred to me that every great team needs an equally great leader," said Deon. "After all, the Justice League has Superman, The Expendables have Sylvester Stallone, and our team has you."

"Save the sales pitch, Deon. While I appreciate the comparison, I'm done with that life. I'm happy here," said Simon.

"Are you really?" asked Deon.

"What?" asked Simon.

"You heard me. You can keep telling yourself that you're happy here acting like Robinson Crusoe, but the fact is you were happiest working for Silhouette. Hell, it's why you accepted Connor's offer to come back in the first place," said Deon.

"Why don't you do it? You're as good as I am at leading," asked Simon.

Deon shrugged. "Yeah… the thing is we need someone who can lead us into hell and bring us back. When we were in Silhouette with Echo 9, you brought us back from every mission, no matter what. You were born for it, man. I wasn't."

Simon knew what he meant. It wasn't an easy thing for the ex-marine to admit, and he knew he was right and not just about leading.

"Besides," said Deon, looking up at him with a wry smile on his face. "The NETWORC is still out there, and with the Triads' resources, we can track them down in the meantime and get revenge for Sheila."

Those last words hit a particular chord with Simon. After she was killed, he swore to kill the leader of the organization that killed her. He had come so close to avenging her, only to be stopped by the man's machinations. This was his chance. With a team like this, he would have the help he needed to find Mr. Zero.

"So what's the word: you in or out, man?" asked Deon.

Simon thought for a minute, letting his words echo in his head. He shifted his gaze to the window at the Aleutian skyline and the promise he made to avenge her death. He also knew what she would do if he had died in that bunker instead of him. It also occurred to him that he would be able to see Mai again.

He looked back at Deon. "Out of curiosity, what's the name of this team of yours?"

"Monkeywrench," answered Deon.

Simon glared at him, wondering if he was serious.

"Don't blame me. Mack came up with it," said Deon.

Simon sighed and pinched the skin between his eye, the patch over his right eye, and the top of his nose.

"According to Mack, it means we throw a Monkeywrench into the plans of the bad guys," said Deon.

"Or it says you're a bunch of incompetent monkeys that don't know what the hell we're doing," said Simon.

"Like I said, I didn't come up with it. So, are you in or not?" Deon asked.

"I'm in. You got yourselves a leader," said Simon. "However, if I'm the leader, there's going to be some rules."

"Like?" asked Deon.

"No innocent people, we only take on jobs that involve taking out bad guys," said Simon.

"Not a problem," said Deon.

"Second, everyone pulls their weight," continued Simon.

"Any more?" asked Deon.

"No, that's it," said Simon.

"Great, because I have my own rule?" said Deon as he stood up. "Shave the beard. You look like a homeless person, and you smell like one, too."

Simon stood up, and the two men looked each other in the eyes for several seconds. "Deal," said Simon as they shook hands.

"Wicked. Now, get your shirt, and let's go. The others are waiting," said Deon.

"Right," muttered Simon as Deon walked outside.

Simon knelt down, pulled the trunk out from under his bed, and carried it outside to the boat. As he put it in the boat, he began to wonder if he had just made a mistake.

Chapter 3
Cold Skies Above

Nigel Solo drove into the parking lot of the MI6 building in London. Dressed in his regular attire of a gray blazer, white dress shirt, gray pants, and black tie, he got out of his car. He quickly ran through the rain and into the building. Upon entering, he walked through the lobby to the elevator. Fortunately, no one else was inside. Nigel placed his palm on the hidden palm print scanner on the segment of the wall above the buttons for the various floors.

After a few minutes, a mechanical voice on the intercom said, "Occupant identified as Nigel Solo, codename: SABRE, field agent of Equinox."

Once the voice was done speaking, the elevator began to move downward for several minutes. Suddenly, it stopped and began moving forward. It stopped again, and the door opened, and Nigel was standing in a small lobby. He walked out of the elevator and glanced upward. In all the years he had been a member of Equinox, he still found it hard to believe that above him were the cold waters of the River Thames.

Brushing the thoughts aside, he walked across the lobby and down several hallways till he reached a wooden door with the words Director on it. Nigel knocked on it and was greeted with a gruff, muffled voice saying, "Come in," from the man inside.

He opened the door and walked into a large, opulent office with bookcases on the walls and a wooden desk in the middle of it. Seated behind the desk was the Director of Equinox, a surly older man named Felix Proffer.

"Good afternoon, Sir," said Nigel.

"Have a seat, SABRE," said Felix, not bothering to look up from the papers in his hands.

Nigel sat down in one of the two chairs in front of the desk. Felix looked up from several papers on his desk and adjusted his glasses.

"I assume you're wondering why I had you return to headquarters," Felix asked.

"I assume it has something to do with Siobhan?" Nigel replied.

"To some degree, it does, since she's involved in it. Regardless, I have some bad news," said Felix. "I'm temporarily canceling the L.A.T. order on Siobhan Costello."

Nigel hid his outrage and confusion as best he could upon hearing Felix's words. "Sir, why? Does the PM know?"

"He approved it. You see, something has come up that is a larger threat to the Crown than her," said Felix.

"What?" asked Nigel.

"Have you ever heard of the Spear of Destiny?" Felix answered.

"Vaguely, Sir, isn't it supposed to be the Spear that was used to pierce the side of Christ during the crucifixion?" said Nigel.

"Well, that's the short version," Felix answered.

"Sir, if I may ask, what Siobhan has to do with it," asked Nigel impatiently.

Felix's eyes narrowed into an angry stare. "SABRE, I understand and sympathize with your reasons for wanting Costello dead, but that is not an excuse to speak to me in that tone."

"My apologies, Sir," said Nigel.

"Forget it. Now, what I'm about to tell you has been classified since the Second World War," said Felix. "As you know, before and during the war, the Nazis scoured the globe for ancient artifacts believing them to be some kind of weapon or some such."

"In 1942, archaeologists belonging to the Germans Aquarius organization found what they believe to be the Spear of Destiny," continued Felix. "The SOE tracked it to Paris, where it was going to be sent to Berlin via train," replied Felix. "Churchill was repulsed at the idea of the Nazis having it, so he ordered us to recover it."

Nigel couldn't believe that this was taking precedence over the assassination order on Siobhan Costello. However, he continued listening impassively so as not to incur his boss's wrath.

"Captain Oliver Stapleton led a team of Equinox agents to recover it in Paris," continued Felix.

"Excuse me, Sir? Do you mean the Oliver Stapleton?" asked Nigel, his attention grabbed by the name.

"Yes, why?" asked Felix.

"I've studied the man's exploits during the war and the Cold War," answered Nigel.

"Good, anyway, they managed to get the Spear and drive to a plane out in the countryside that would fly them back here," replied Felix. "However, the plane crashed in the channel, and only Stapleton survived."

"As for the Spear, it was lost…until now, that is," continued Felix.

"What happened?" asked Nigel.

"Several weeks ago, a Swiss diving team found it by accident and sold it to an artifact collector living in Australia," said Felix. "This collector was then contacted by Aquarius, who convinced him to sell it to them."

"So?" asked Nigel.

"Due to its political and religious value, we cannot allow Aquarius to possess the Spear, so the PM has ordered us to recover it by any means necessary," answered Felix.

"Where does Siobhan factor in?" asked Nigel.

Felix sighed, knowing that was the most important part of this assignment to him. "Obviously, we cannot send our own people to get it. Luckily, a new PMC has sprung up on Sankan led by one of our old friends from Langley…with Siobhan as a member."

Nigel thought about who he meant by a friend from Langley when suddenly it occurred to him.

"Simon Kane?" said Nigel.

"No, Deon Bowman," replied Felix.

Nigel raised his left eyebrow in surprise.

"We believe him, Siobhan and two others have been looking for him after some fight in North Korea," explained Felix.

"I'm surprised, I thought he was dead. Still, after what happened in Iceland, Siobhan is most likely a member," said Nigel, who was starting to piece together Felix's plan.

"Exactly, we haven't contacted them about the job offer yet since we lack the details about how it's being transported," said Felix.

"So…what's my role in all this?" asked Nigel.

"Once we find out how it's being transported, you will go to Sankan and contact them," answered Felix.

"In the meantime, I have a separate mission for you," said Felix.

"Oh?" said Nigel, surprised.

"Yes, I want you to go to Birkenhead and find out what you can from Stapleton," said Felix as he handed Nigel a piece of paper with an address on it.

"Odds are he won't know anything of use. Still, it couldn't hurt to check," continued Felix as Nigel slid the paper into his pocket.

"Sir, I'm curious, though. This sounds like something Disciple 13 might be involved with also," said Nigel.

Felix grunted at the mention of the Vatican's black ops agency, which Equinox had clashed with in the past.

"We've been keeping an eye on them, and according to what we've been able to find out, they're aware of the situation as well," said Felix.

"As to whether they will try to get it is unknown," continued Felix.

"How do you think they'll react, Sir?" asked Nigel.

"Personally, I think they'll either send someone or hire someone to get it, then again, when it comes to them," answered Felix.

"Expect the unexpected, Sir," interrupted Nigel with a grin.

"Quite," replied Felix. "However, we believe someone else is interested in the Spear?"

"Who?" asked Nigel.

"Since last year, someone has been attacking Aquarius operatives all over the globe," answered Felix. "We don't know who this individual is, but we're investigating. Personally, I suspect Guild involvement."

"Is anyone else involved in this?" Nigel asked.

"Not particularly. The only people who care about this enough to actually do something are us, Aquarius, Disciple 13, and possibly the

Israelis. But they're too busy playing tag with ISIS and Hamas to care about this," answered Felix.

Nigel thought about what Felix had said. It made sense. Still, he couldn't help but ask the question that had been nagging at him.

"What about Siobhan when this is over?" asked Nigel.

"We'll see, anyway, you're dismissed," answered Felix.

"Yes, Sir," said Nigel as he stood up and walked out of the office.

Once the door had closed behind him, he punched the wall out of anger. He felt outraged at the fact that he would now have to work with a terrorist like Siobhan. As his calm returned, he laughed at the irony that now she would be working for the very country she had attacked. He shrugged and walked to the elevator, deciding that having to work with Siobhan was a far lesser evil compared to Aquarius.

Chapter 4
Gangsters Paradise

After a short layover in Russia, followed by a transfer to a private jet, Deon said the Triad had loaned them. Simon, Mack, Deon, and Siobhan were on the way back to Sankan Island. Simon was in the plane's bathroom. It was cramped with a shower on the side. Simon looked at his reflection in the mirror, his bearded, disheveled face staring back at him in the reflection. He picked up the shaver next to the faucet and began shaving off the beard.

As he shaved, he had to admit it he was surprised that they hadn't changed: Siobhan Costello, a beautiful former I.R.A. assassin turned Catholic nun, was still wearing her black and white nun's habit and as quiet as ever with her long red hair. Mack Roycewicz, a tall American man with a large, muscular frame and unkempt blonde hair, was wearing an ugly red and green Hawaiian shirt and khaki pants.

After a few minutes, Simon's long beard was gone, and he then picked up the scissors and began cutting his hair, which was down to his shoulders. He had to admit it was nice to see them all again. Maybe Deon was right, thought

Simon as he cut his hair. It suddenly occurred to him that they hadn't told him about what happened to Mai, Deng, and everyone else on the island since he left. With his hair back to its normal length, he got in the shower and turned on the water.

After six months on Agattu, he had forgotten how reinvigorating a hot shower felt. When he was done, he turned off the water and returned to the mirror. He opened a small jar of hair gel and smoothed his hair back until it was flat. Hanging from a hook on the door were his dark blue trench coat, black shirt, cross-draw shoulder holster, and dark green pants. His gun and wrist blade were in the cockpit with the pilot and Deon for safety. He quickly put them on.

Simon looked at himself in the mirror and felt pleased with his reflection. He took a deep breath and walked out of the bathroom into the plane's cabin. It was an ornate, large room with leather couches on the left and right sides and a reclining chair next to the left couch. Mack was sitting on the couch on the left, looking at his phone, while Siobhan was sitting on the other couch reading her Bible. They looked up at Simon as he walked out of the bathroom.

"Finally, the beard is gone," said Mack sarcastically.

"You're just sore you couldn't grow one," said Simon sarcastically as he sat down in the reclining chair.

"So…I have some questions," said Simon as he leaned back in the chair.

"Shoot," said Mack.

"Ignoring for a minute how you found me, I'm curious what's happened since I've been gone?" asked Simon.

"Well, for starters, Ukraine and Russia are still at war," said Mack sarcastically.

"Yeah, I kind of figured that out already," replied Simon drily.

"Seriously, though, what did I miss?" asked Simon as he reclined in the chair.

Mack and Siobhan looked at each other, then back at Simon. "Where do we start?" asked Mack.

"With Mai," said Simon.

"Well, she's still alive and kicking for starters," Mack said.

"Good," said Simon, relieved.

After North Korea, we brought her back to Sankan since her father thought it would be the safest place for her. When we told her that we were going to try to find you, she wanted to come with us, but her father said no and forbade any of the Triad from letting her leave Sankan," said Mack.

"So she decided to work in the Triads office and help whenever she can," said Siobhan. "She's even joined me in the soup kitchen."

"She always was the charitable type," said Simon. Even though he had known her for a while now, it was still hard to believe that the most dangerous woman on Earth was a Catholic Nun.

"So what about Deng?" asked Simon.

"He's fine, just has to walk with a cane now," Mack answered.

"So, I'm guessing Sankan is still as shitty as ever?" asked Simon.

"Yeah, the Triads managed to repair the damage from the NETWORC's last attack," Mack answered.

"Good to know," said Simon.

He was about to ask the question he had occasionally asked himself on the island. However, before anyone could speak, Deon's booming voice came over the intercom.

"Lady and gentlemen, we are now beginning our descent to the airport," said Deon.

Simon, Mack, and Siobhan looked out windows that lined the sides of the plane. The waters of the Devil's Sea soon gave way to

Sankan Island. In the distance, they could see the small mountain range of Sankan, with the volcanic Mount Soka looming over the island. Not far from the airport was the skyline of the small city on the island's southern half. The city was nothing more than row after row of dilapidated slums inhabited by the island's small population of the forgotten, the desperate, and the damned.

Ruling over this empire of sin was the local offices of the Vasilev Syndicate from Russia and the Heise She Li Triad from China. They ruled from two skyscrapers across the street from each other. The small hook-shaped harbor held several freighters belonging to the Triad or the Syndicate, as well as several small fishing boats that belonged to the island's fishermen. Due to various political disputes in the Philippine Sea, Sankan was claimed by no country. As a result, it had become a haven for fugitives, organized crime, and people with nowhere else to go.

The plane landed at the airport and skidded to a stop. Deon and the pilot walked out of the cockpit and opened the door. Simon, Mack, Deon, and Siobhan walked down the steps out of the plane. To Simon's surprise, a black SUV was waiting for them.

Simon looked at Mack, "Triad?" said Simon.

"Yep, they've agreed to help us get set up," said Mack.

"Right," said Simon as they walked to the cars, and they got in.

"Wait till you see the HQ," said Mack.

"And the surprise," said Deon as the car drove away from the airport.

Chapter 5
New Digs

After a half-hour drive through the city streets of Sankan, they arrived at a large, dilapidated two-floor mansion. The building was covered in residue from black smoke, bullet holes, and fire. Several windows were broken. However, some parts of them looked like they had been fixed. In front of the building was a large, unkempt lawn with a cement fence and gate between the mansion and the rest of the city. Cutting across the lawn was a thin stone driveway that ended in a circle at the front door.

"Welcome to the Boom Factory!" said Mack proudly as they drove up to the front door.

Simon shrugged at the name, "The Boom Factory? Really?"

"What? It's got a good ring to it," protested Mack dismissively.

"According to who?" replied Simon sardonically.

"Believe me, there were worse ones, but that was the best one," said Deon. "Hell, if you think that's bad, wait until you hear the slogan he came up with."

"Do I even want to know?" asked Simon.

"If you got the bills, we got the skills," Mack answered with a smug grin.

Simon turned and looked at him. "It's not that bad, but Monkeywrench, really? You had worse names than that?"

"Much worse," Deon grunted.

"There's a reason for it?" asked Simon.

"Yeah, same reason why the place looks like hammered shit," answered Mack. "Last April, someone blew up half of the place."

Last April? That was during the Triads' war with the cartel, thought Simon as they pulled up to the mansion. As they got out of the car, Simon noticed a large square-shaped building next to the mansion.

"That's the garage slash armory," said Deon, pointing to it.

"Believe it or not, Deng told me this place used to belong to the Rojas cartels' boss after the Triad and the syndicate kicked them out," explained Mack.

"I can believe it," replied Simon as they walked to the front door. He remembered watching the explosion from a distance.

"So, how'd we get it then?" asked Simon.

"The Russians didn't know what to do with it, so they sold it to us," answered Deon. "Ever since, the Triad has been helping us refurbish it."

"We've got power, AC, plumbing, a fully stocked armory, kitchen, garage, and a helipad with a Blackhawk in the back, and finally a boat dock with a patrol boat," said Mack.

"Impressive, where'd you get a Blackhawk?" asked Simon.

"We bought one from Demir," answered Deon as Simon noticed a small garden in the front yard.

"Whose is that?" asked Simon, pointing to it.

"Mine," answered Siobhan with a proud smile.

"Oh yeah, I forgot Siobhan's trying to turn the front yard into a massive garden for food and shit," explained Mack.

"Anything good in there?" asked Simon.

"Mostly fruits and vegetables," Siobhan answered.

"Good, very good," said Simon.

"Wait till you see the inside," said Mack as he began to open the door.

"But first," said Deon as he turned towards the garage. Simon and the others followed him to the garage.

Must be my surprise, Simon thought as Deon lifted the garage door up, revealing a large room. Its walls were filled with racks of guns, tools, and boxes of various types of ammunition.

However, what caught Simon's attention was the motorcycle in the middle.

"Is that what I think it is?" said Simon as he pointed at it.

"Yep," said Deon. "It's a Cobra Streetrod, Slashdown 1911B."

"Beautiful bike," said Simon. "My surprise, I assume?"

"Uh-huh. I know you like these things. Figured it would sweeten the deal," replied Deon as he handed Simon the keys.

"It certainly does. Where'd you get it?" asked Simon.

"Russians," Deon answered. "I've made some modifications to it, specifically a compartment for a pistol and a souped-up engine."

"Very nice," answered Simon as he studied the bike.

"Wait until you see the rest of the factory," said Deon.

"Lead the way," replied Simon as he put the keys in his pocket.

Mack opened the door on the left side of the garage, and they walked into a once opulent foyer with a large ornate staircase in the center. The staircase led to a balcony overlooking the foyer. On the far right and left sides of the staircase were two halls that led to several rooms. Simon followed Deon, Mack, and Siobhan to a room on the right side of the staircase. Several television sets adorned the walls, each showing various news channels, while some displayed computer data. In the middle of the room was a messy desk with two desktop computers and keyboards. Simon noticed an ashtray next to the keyboard with what looked like a lit joint in it.

There were several folding chairs in the room around the desk. In a swivel chair behind the desk was a disheveled man in a white dress shirt, gray pants, and black tie with glasses.

"Yo Dennis! What's up?" yelled Mack as they walked in.

Instantly, the man spun around and stood up. Simon recognized him instantly as Dennis Faraday. "Welcome back, Simon," said Dennis as the two men shook hands.

"Dennis, here is our computer specialist and logistical support," said Mack.

"That must be why he's in the room with all the computers," observed Simon sarcastically.

"Consider it the briefing room, man," said Dennis.

Simon noticed that he was more relaxed than he was the last time he saw him, and then he saw the ash tray on the desk next to a keyboard. "What's with that?" he asked, pointing at it.

Mack slung his arm around Dennis. "Mr. Faraday here has discovered the soothing power of Miss Mary Jane," said Mack with a cocky smile.

"I see, well, as long as it doesn't affect your work, I don't care," said Simon sternly.

"It hasn't so far," said Deon.

"Thanks, it actually makes me even more focused," Dennis replied.

"Whatever works," grunted Simon.

"Anyway, Simon, your rooms are upstairs with the rest of them," said Mack, pointing to the ceiling.

"By the way, here's your stuff," said Deon as he handed Simon his pistol and wrist blade.

"Thanks, I felt naked without these," said Simon as he took them.

He placed the pistol in his holster and clipped the wrist blade to his right wrist. The wrist blade consisted of a small, tight metal armband. When he flicked his wrist back, a knife popped out of the armband.

"So what do you think?" asked Mack.

"I must admit, it's certainly impressive," said Simon.

"Tell me about it. It's just like old times," said Deon.

"Let's hope not," quipped Simon wryly. "I'd like a more in-depth tour of the place later, as well as a briefing on our technical capabilities."

"I can handle that," said Dennis.

"Right now, though, we need to talk," said Simon as he sat down in one of the chairs.

Deon, Siobhan, Dennis, and Mack sat down in the chairs as well, curious as to the topic.

"Mack and Siobhan filled me in about Mai, the Triad, and the rest. However, I have one more question," said Simon. "What about the NETWORC?"

The question had been gnawing at him for months. They looked nervous at the question, "What?" asked Simon.

"The truth is, between setting up Monkeywrench and tracking you down, we haven't been able to keep tabs on them," answered Dennis.

Simon was about to speak when Mack interjected. "However, Deng told us that the Triad was looking into them, but they've heard nothing since TREADWATER."

"In fact, considering our limited capabilities, we won't be able to either," said Dennis.

"Still, we can work with what we have," Siobhan noted.

"Besides, you killed their leader, right?" asked Deon.

Simon shrugged, remembering his showdown at TREADWATER with Mr. Zero. "That's…..complicated."

"His name is Jonas Oscar Mannheim, goes by the name Mr. Zero," sighed Simon.

They looked at him in surprise at his answer. "He knew I was coming to kill him, so he had the NETWORC plant a suitcase nuke somewhere in the world that is keyed to his heartbeat," explained Simon.

"So if his heart stops beating, then a city gets destroyed?" asked Dennis.

Simon nodded in response.

"Hardcore," said Mack.

"And insane," observed Deon.

"Wait…if you didn't kill him, then what did you do?" asked Mack.

"I broke his arms and legs, but I don't know if he's still alive," answered Simon bluntly.

"Brutal," grunted Mack.

"Hold on a minute," said Dennis as he reached for his tablet on his desk.

"What are you doing?" asked Siobhan as Dennis typed away on his computer.

"That name….Jonas Mannheim, it sounds familiar," said Dennis.

He finished typing and held up the tablet. On the screen was a picture of a handsome blonde man in a suit giving a speech at a charity event. "This him?" asked Dennis.

"Yeah. I'd recognize the bastard anywhere," grunted Simon. He noticed that the picture was dated last month, confirming that he did survive after all.

"It says he's the CEO of a company called Kronos International," said Dennis.

"I don't care if he's the Pope. The son of a bitch dies," said Simon.

As he said the words, Simon noticed Siobhan raise an eyebrow at the mention of the Pope. "No offense, Siobhan."

"None taken," replied Siobhan with a smile.

"So what's the plan?" asked Deon.

"My plan is to find a way to disable the detonator and take him out," said Simon. "Perhaps the Triad and Syndicate can help."

"We can ask Deng about that. They are our best ally against these guys," said Deon.

Simon sensed that they were dancing around an issue. "Ok, what friends and enemies do we have here?"

"Well, the Triad and Syndicate won't bother us as long as we don't mess with them. However, the Triad does like us more after we rescued Mai," explained Deon.

"It's the same deal with the Heartbreak Hotel and the Love Shack," said Mack.

"The who?" Simon asked, having never heard the names.

"Two rival gangs of prostitutes, one's Russian, one's Korean," explained Deon. "Not much of a threat, but Love Shack has connections with the Vasilev Syndicate."

"And then there's the Smiling Boys," said Dennis.

"Common street punks scared shitless of the Triad, the Russians, and anyone connected with them," Deon said.

"Anyone else?" asked Simon.

"Well, there's the Flying Fish Trading Company," explained Mack.

"The mercs that helped us after the NETWORC attacked the Triad, right?" said Simon.

"That's them. They used to be the top mercs on the island, but they aren't happy about having to compete with us," Mack explained.

"Well, they can deal with it," grunted Simon.

"They do have this smoking hot Cuban chick on their team, though," he said slyly.

"Didn't she sucker punch you last week?" Deon asked.

"I thought I had a chance," said Mack with a shrug.

"Woman's crazy, Mack, be careful. What if we need weapons and ammo?"

"If we need anything like that, there's Noam, a cranky Israeli dude who set up shop in the Russian sector. If we need more ammo or new guns, he can get it," answered Deon.

"Thought arms dealers weren't allowed on Sankan?" asked Simon.

"Russians made sure Noam was an exception. Really, they just don't want your old girlfriend doing business here," Deon explained.

Simon rolled his eyes at Deon's sarcastic mention of Gretchen.

"Finally, there's the Nazis," said Mack with disgust in his voice.

"The what?" Simon asked in surprise.

"He's talking about an Aquarius bunker in the forest north of the city. Bastards mostly keep to themselves. However, they do come into the city to buy guns to ship back to Argentina," explained Deon.

He yawned. "I'm going to bed. I'm still tired from the flight," said Simon as he stood up.

"I'll show you where your room is," said Deon as he stood.

"Lead the way," said Simon as he followed Deon up the stairs.

"By the way, we have a meeting with Deng and Mai tomorrow!" yelled Dennis.

"Got it," said Simon as they walked up the staircase. Simon followed Deon to the top of the staircase and then down a hallway to a door with the words "Simon Kane" written on it with a black Sharpie.

"Here you are," said Deon.

Simon opened the door and walked into a small room with a bed, closet, shelf, and table and chair in it.

"Not exactly the Ritz, is it?" said Simon.

All he heard in response was the door closing behind him. He turned around and saw Deon looking at him, his arms crossed. "So what do you think?"

"I'm impressed at what you've set up here, Deon," said Simon.

"Knew it," said Deon proudly. "In addition to everything else, I've been putting them through various combat simulations, so they should fight even better than they did in North Korea."

"Guess we'll see," said Simon, curious to see how they performed in the field.

"Anyway, get some sleep. We've got a big day tomorrow," said Deon as he turned towards the door and opened it.

"You too," said Simon as Deon walked out of the room and closed the door behind him.

Simon got undressed and went to bed, trying not to think about tomorrow.

Chapter 6
From Hell Below

Established in 1938 and answering directly to Adolf Hitler, Aquarius was a covert division of the German SS specializing in black operations. When the Third Reich's downfall became inevitable, the organization's members fled to a secret compound constructed in the remote jungles of Argentina, codenamed VALHALLA, for just such an eventuality. In the years following the war, Aquarius had dedicated itself to getting revenge on the allies, the destruction of Israel, and the creation of a global Fourth Reich. Using ten million dollars worth of gold stolen from the Reichsbank before the end of the war, they established themselves as a terrorist organization with cells across the world.

The nightmare was always the same for Friedrich Zacharias the third. He was surrounded by fire and death, the Aquarius Empire in flames, and walking out of the flames was a woman and a snarling dog. She was clad in black with one eye and blonde hair; she had a seductive figure and death in her eye as he approached him with a pistol in her hand. Zacharias was lying on his back too hurt to move. As this woman approached him, she aimed the gun at his head as he struggled to realize why she looked so familiar, and then, just as she pulled the trigger, he woke up.

He sat up in his bed to find himself once again in his room. Outside, he heard his men doing their morning exercises in the courtyard. He rubbed his face, asking himself for the hundredth time why he kept having these dreams and what they meant. He hadn't asked anyone since there could be no weakness in Aquarius, especially not from its leader and especially not from his bloodline. Suddenly, there was a knock on the door. Zacharias sighed, stood up, and put on his bathrobe, yelling, "Enter."

Into the room walked his assistant Christoph, a bald, sour-faced man dressed in black. Before he spoke, he raised his right arm to his neck so it was parallel to his head, straightened the hand, making it parallel to his arm, and yelled, "Seig Heil."

Zacharias, the leader of Aquarius, returned his salute casually, and Christoph lowered his arm and approached the desk. "Sir, I have new information on Operation SPEERSPITZE."

"I'm sure you do," replied Zacharias smugly.

"The Australian has agreed to give us the artifact," Christoph explained.

"People tend to capitulate when you threaten their family," said Zacharias dryly.

"The Spear will be transported here via the Eva," said Christoph, ignoring his sarcasm.

"It would be better if we could fly it," grumbled Zacharias.

"I agree, Sir, but we lack sufficient aircraft for transport," said Christoph. "Besides, Eva is very well-defended."

"True, anything else?" asked Zacharias.

"Yes, actually, we've tracked down one of the British agents who stole it in 1942," answered Christoph. "Apparently, he's living alone in Birkenhead. What do you wish us to do about him?"

Zacharias thought for a minute. "We have a cell in England, right?"

"Yes, Sir, in Liverpool," Christoph answered.

"Have him killed. Think of it as payback for stealing what was rightfully ours," said Zacharias.

"We could try asking Vogel for?" Christoph began

As soon as he said the name, Zacharias glared at him harshly, and he knew to drop the subject lest he face harsh punishment.

"I'll contact our people in Liverpool immediately," said Christoph quickly.

"See that you do," grunted Zacharias, the sneer on his face slowly fading. Are we any closer to determining who's been attacking our men?"

"Regrettably, Sir, there's nothing," answered Christoph.

"It doesn't matter, though. Once we have the Spear, the world will be ours," Zacharias noted. He looked over at Christoph, "You're dismissed."

Christoph nodded and walked out of the office. Once he was gone, Zacharias was alone with his thoughts and the memory of that dream. He sighed and shook his head in a desperate attempt to purge it from his mind and get on with the day's business.

*****

By the time Nigel Solo arrived at the address Felix had given him, it was a night out. He got out of the car and looked around the neighborhood. It consisted of rows and rows of identical houses with three floors. He had parked in front of the house. He walked up three steps to the front door and knocked several times.

After receiving no answer, he looked around, and after seeing no one was around, he reached into his pocket and pulled out a small lockpick. He slid it into the keyhole, and after a few minutes of careful manipulations, the door opened. He smiled as he returned the lock pick to his pocket. Quietly, he walked inside and closed the door behind him. The house was pitch black and quiet except for the blue light and the noise of a television coming from the living room.

Upon entering the living room, Nigel turned on the lights and saw the sleeping body of Oliver Stapleton lying in a reclining chair. He had short white hair and, hanging from his neck, was a pair of reading glasses. He was wearing a white sleeveless shirt and boxer shorts. Nigel noticed he vaguely resembled Michael Caine. Nigel turned around and switched off the television. As soon as he turned it off, he heard the unmistakable click of a gun being cocked from behind him.

"I was watching that," said Stapleton in a surly, cockney accent.

Chapter 7
Bedtime Story

"Turn around slowly," said Stapleton.

Nigel held up his hands and turned around so he was facing Stapleton. He sat up in his chair, aiming an Enfield Mk 2 revolver at Nigel's head. "I must say you punks are dressing much nicer these days," said Stapleton as he noticed Nigel's gray suit.

"It helps to dress for success," said Nigel wryly.

Stapleton grinned slightly at the joke, "your obviously not some hooligan, so what the bloody hell do you want?"

"I want to ask you some questions," Nigel answered.

"Of course you do. Who's asking those questions?" replied Stapleton.

Nigel thought carefully about how to answer the question. "My name is SABRE. I'm with Equinox."

Stapleton lowered his pistol upon hearing the word Equinox. "Fancy some tea?" asked Stapleton.

"Yes, if you insist," replied Nigel.

Stapleton stood up and walked to the kitchen. Nigel followed him. By the time he arrived in the kitchen, Stapleton had already prepared two cups of tea. He handed one of the cups to Nigel and sat down at the wooden table in the center of the kitchen. He took a sip of tea and sat down at the table across from Stapleton. He noticed Stapleton's revolver was on the table, not far from his hand. Stapleton took a long sip of tea, his eyes locked on Nigel.

"So this is what Equinox's field men look like now? I must say I'm not impressed," Stapleton observed.

"Glad to have your approval," said Nigel sarcastically as he took a sip of tea.

"Don't get sarcastic with me, you little shite. I was fighting for the crown when you were still watching Thomas the bloody tank engine," sneered Stapleton.

"So I've heard," replied Nigel.

"Anyway, what the bloody hell does Equinox want with me?" asked Stapleton crassly.

"Operation: BLOOD PIRATE," answered Nigel.

Stapleton's face went white at Nigel's words, "If we're going down this road, I'm going to need something stronger than tea," said Stapleton with a weary sigh.

He stood up, walked over to the refrigerator, pulled out a bottle of Guinness, poured it into his teacup then sat down. He closed his eyes, then drank the tea, and looked directly at Nigel. He could tell Stapleton was sizing him up.

"What do you want to know?" asked Stapleton.

"For starters, how did you survive the plane crash?" Nigel asked.

"No idea. Me, Talbot, and Barlow were in the plane flying across the channel when Barlow dropped the box on the floor, causing the bloody thing to break open, and then we saw it," began Stapleton.

He took another sip of Guinness. "It was Talbot, the academic, who was the first to pick it up, and then it started to glow. The next thing we knew, the engines stopped, and we were going down."

"I woke up on a fishing boat that picked me up while en route back to England. Sadly, Talbot and Barlow didn't make it."

"It glowed?" said Nigel, raising his eyebrow in surprise.

"More than that. It caused our plane to crash. I'm bloody certain of it," replied Stapleton. "Now, why the sudden interest in it?"

"We have reason to believe Aquarius might have found it," answered Nigel.

"I'm not surprised. Himmler made finding it a top priority for Zacharias," said Stapleton.

He took another long drink of Guinness. "Listen to me carefully. You cannot let those bastards get the Spear," said Stapleton.

"I've seen some crazy things over the years…but the Spear, there's something about it," said Stapleton, a haunted look coming across his wrinkled face. "I'm not superstitious, but the Spear is…unearthly."

Before Nigel could reply, they heard the front door of the house being kicked open, followed by several men running inside. Nigel instinctively pulled out his pistol, a 7.65mm Walther PPK, while Stapleton picked up his revolver. They stood up and ran into the living room and saw three bald men dressed in black holding Uzis and shotguns, looking around. As Nigel and Stapleton entered the room, the three men turned and aimed their guns at them.

"Bloody bastards!" yelled Nigel as he fired three shots at them with his revolver. The three men fell over dead, and Nigel noticed the swastikas tattooed on their arms.

"Come into my house, will you?" barked Stapleton smugly.

Nigel looked out the window and then jumped to the ground at what he saw. "Stapleton, get down!"

Before Stapleton could respond, machine gun bullets ripped through the house, hitting Stapleton. Nigel crawled over to the window and saw the van the gunfire was coming from. He aimed his pistol at it and fired several shots, and then the firing stopped.

Nigel crawled towards Stapleton's lifeless, immobile body, praying he was okay.

"Stapleton, are you okay?" asked Nigel as he turned his body over.

"Call me Sir, you wanker," he answered weakly as he tried to stop the bleeding.

He coughed weakly as blood came up from his throat. With his last remaining ounce of strength, Stapleton grabbed Nigel's jacket and pulled him toward him. "Listen to me, do not let those bastards get the Spear…you have to destroy it….the damn thing wasn't meant for this world," said Stapleton fiercely.

Before Nigel could respond, Stapleton lost consciousness, and his body went limp. Nigel closed Stapleton's eyes and glanced outside just as the firing resumed. He waited until they stopped firing, then jumped up from cover. He fired one shot, and the van suddenly exploded.

Surprised at the explosion, he walked outside as the once-dark neighborhood was illuminated by the dancing flames.

He looked around, trying to find who had destroyed the truck. Suddenly, a red sports car pulled up in front of him. The window rolled down, and Nigel saw a beautiful blonde woman with a black eye patch over her right eye. She was dressed in black pants, a jacket, and a dark red shirt.

"Sasha, what the bloody hell are you doing here?" asked Nigel, stunned at seeing her.

"Get in now!" yelled Sasha. Nigel could hear the Sirens approaching police cars in the distance.

"Whatever you say," grunted Nigel as he got in the seat next to Sasha.

Once he was inside, Sasha drove away from the scene. Nigel noticed a small single-shot grenade launcher on the floor in front of him. Before he could ask a question, Sasha pulled out a small pistol and fired it at Nigel's arm. Instinctively, he looked down at his arm and saw a dart sticking out. He tried to speak, but he felt his consciousness fading away. Sasha put the pistol in her pocket, jammed her foot on the pedal, and drove off.

Chapter 8
An Old Friend

Simon awoke to a loud knocking on the door of his room. Still groggy from sleep, he got up and quickly got dressed before answering the door.

Upon answering the door, he saw Deon standing in the doorway. "Dude, let's go, we've got that meeting."

"What time is it?" asked Simon as he rubbed his face, still trying to wake up.

"Time to go, c'mon. The others are waiting in the car downstairs," replied Deon.

Simon shrugged and followed Mack out of the mansion to a black SUV parked in front of the mansion. Deon and Simon joined Mack, Dennis, and Siobhan in the back of the car. Once inside, the driver pulled away from the mansion and drove down the battered streets of Sankan. As they drove across the city, they looked out the window.

Simon and the others had seen poverty-stricken hellholes across the world, but Sankan was different. The suffering of the people who tried to eke out a living on the island was made all the more tragic because many of them had come to Sankan having nowhere else to go. In addition to the illicit activities that they carried out on Sankan and abroad, the Triad and syndicate maintained several kitchens and services for the people, such as water and power. They did this so they could prevent an uprising amongst the people. In the center of the island were two buildings that seemed to touch the sky itself across the street from each other, the local offices of the Triad and syndicate.

Decades ago, they had divided control of the island's city in half. One half belonged to the Syndicate, the other to the Triad. The only exceptions were the airport and the harbor, which they both used and therefore considered neutral. Simon and the others pulled up in front of the Triad's building. The driver opened the door, and they stepped out of the car.

They looked up at the Triads building; it was a typical-looking light brown colored skyscraper. On the roof was a smaller structure with a red pagoda atop it. There was also a heliport and a garden on the roof. Across the street was the headquarters of the Vasilev Syndicate, which was an unimpressive gray skyscraper of the same height. Seeing the two buildings reminded Dennis of the office buildings that littered the skyline of New York.

The driver escorted them inside and, after surrendering their weapons, was told to take the elevator to Deng's office in the Pagoda. They got in the elevator, and after a short ride, the doors opened. They stepped into a long hallway where an assistant was waiting for them. The assistant walked them to Deng's office. Simon thanked the assistant and opened the door to Deng's office. His office was a large room with a red carpet and bookcases on the walls.

On the other side of the room, facing them, were six chairs in front of a wooden desk. As they entered, the chair behind the desk spun around, revealing Deng. He was a tall, handsome, yet rugged-faced Chinese man of medium build, dressed in a black trench coat, black tie, white dress shirt, and black pants. He had been chosen by the Triad's leader, known as the Mountain Master, to oversee the Triad's operations on the island.

"Welcome back, Simon, how was your vacation?" asked Deng.

"Cold," grunted Simon as they sat down in front of the desk.

"Alaska usually is, from what I hear," Deng replied wryly.

"Why are we here, Deng? They told me everything had already been set up," Simon asked.

"Americans are blunt as ever, first to go over the remaining information and second," said Deng.

Before he could finish, the doors flung open. Into the office ran a slender, attractive Chinese woman with long black hair and glasses. She was dressed in blue jeans and a short-sleeved dress shirt. "Simon!" yelled the woman.

"That's why," said Deng as she ran towards him.

"Hey Mai," said Simon softly as he stood up. He was surprised to see her on Sankan, of all places.

She embraced him, almost knocking him off balance. "I'm so glad to see you."

"Me too, Mai," said Simon as he held her in his arms and closed his eyes.

"I knew you were still alive," said Mai softly as tears began to appear in her eyes.

"Ahem!" barked Deng. Mai and Simon suddenly remembered where they were. They let go of each other and sat down.

"Now then, like you said, everything has already been set up, but I felt it best to explain the details to you since you're the head of it," said Deng.

"Monkeywrench has approval from both us and the Russians to operate as private contractors on Sankan, just like Flying Fish does," continued Deng. "However, if you're going to play in our sandbox, you will play by our rules."

"For starters, you are on your own unless we have hired you. There is no support, backup, or funding from us or the Russians," said Deng.

"No support, no backup or cash...nothing new," replied Simon sarcastically.

"We have agreed to act as...a bank for you, but that is the limit of our involvement," said Deng. "However, because of what you have done for us and for Mai, the Mountain Master has decided to extend to you the Ninety-Nine Favors."

"Whoa," replied Mack.

"What's that?" asked Dennis.

"It is the biggest reward that we can give someone who has done a great service for us. You can ask us for ninety-nine favors, and we will do everything in our power to accomplish them for nothing in return," answered Deng.

"So...how many favors do we have left?" asked Dennis.

"Ninety-seven," answered Deng. "Use them wisely," he said, looking up at Simon.

"Good to know," replied Simon.

"Also, make sure you pick your jobs carefully because we make better friends than enemies. Same with the Russians across the street," Deng advised.

"I'll bet, so do you have a job for us then?" asked Simon.

Deng shrugged. "At the moment, no, but we have referred you to our contacts across the globe, so you should expect a job shortly."

"Not to mention the Guild," said Mack.

They looked at him as he spoke curiously. "I've taken the liberty of registering us as a freelance outfit with the International Assassins Guild, so they'll contact us pretty soon," spoke Mack.

"That's it for the most part, any questions?" Deng asked.

"What's Mai doing here?" asked Simon.

"I've decided to stay on the island as Deng's assistant …and to provide relief for the people," she answered, annoyed at being spoken to like she wasn't there.

"Is that a problem?" asked Mai with a smile as she looked directly at Simon.

"Not at all," said Simon, smiling back at her.

"I suspect you two have some catching up to do. Me and the others will go over the remaining paperwork," Deng said.

"Want to go for a walk, Simon?" asked Mai as she stood up.

Simon could tell the others had no objections, so he stood up. "Let me know when you're done."

"Got it, boss," said Deon.

Simon followed Mai out of the office to the garden outside. Once they were outside, Mai swung around and punched Simon in the chin. He had been hit harder, but he usually knew the reason.

"Quite a punch. Have you been training?" asked Simon as he looked back at her.

"Deng's been teaching me how to fight," answered Mai.

"Clearly, you're a good student," quipped Simon as he rubbed his chin.

"Why did you leave?" asked Mai angrily.

Simon had been expecting this ever since he found out Mai was still alive on the island. He sighed, "After what happened in North Korea, I felt the safest place for you would be away from me," said Simon.

"This has to do with Sheila, doesn't it?" asked Mai.

Mai could tell by Simon's silence that she was right. "I understand, really I do. You're afraid I'll wind up like her, right?"

"Pretty much yeah," replied Simon.

"I must be pretty special to you if you're willing to go to the ends of the earth," said Mai.

Simon placed his hand on Mai's shoulder, and she looked up at him. "You and Sheila were the only women I've ever truly loved."

"That is so corny," Mai replied as she laughed softly.

"I thought it sounded romantic," said Simon with a grin.

"So where do we go from here?" asked Mai.

Simon shrugged his shoulders. "Let's take it slow and see what happens."

"Alright," said Mai with a smile.

They hugged each other, "I guess we'll see each other around the island," said Simon as he held her.

Mai looked up at him as their eyes met, "Works for me," as they let each other go, "You want a tour?"

"Depends, you going to slug me again?" asked Simon.

"Maybe," said Mai sarcastically as she walked towards the door.

"My kind of odds," replied Simon as he shrugged his shoulders and followed Mai inside.

Chapter 9
Necessary Evils

Nigel Solo awoke in a small windowless room on a bed. He sat up and discovered that his gun, wallet, and phone were gone. The room consisted of a bed, a table, and two chairs. Before he could think of what to do next, Sasha walked into the room. Sasha was a unique kind of person, all too willing to kill for money. Nigel read in the file Equinox had on her that after leaving the black ops Russian intelligence agency known as Red Curtain, she became a mercenary for hire.

He had encountered her only a handful of times over the years. Most of what he knew came from a friend of his who had more encounters with her. Nigel made sure to keep his guard up around her because, despite how beautiful she was, she was one of the deadliest assassins on the planet.

"Sasha Molotova," growled Nigel.

"Nice to see you too, Nigel," said Sasha sarcastically in her seductive Russian accent. "I'm sorry for tranquilizing you, but I couldn't risk you finding out the location of this safe house."

"Mind telling me why you did it in the first place?" Nigel asked.

"Because we have a common enemy," answered Sasha.

"Aquarius?" replied Nigel, curious as to how.

"Last April, while on a job in Sankan, I came across a disc containing information related to Aquarius's leader," said Sasha. "Ever since, I've been trying to find him, but the trail went cold."

"However, I tracked one of their people to Austria, and after some…convincing, he told me about the Spear," she continued.

"Which led you here?" said Nigel.

"Yes, to an Aquarius cell in London," Sasha answered.

"And after some more 'convincing, ' they told you about Stapleton," said Nigel.

Sasha nodded. So Sasha's the one who's been terrorizing Aquarius all this time, thought Nigel.

"One question, though, how did you know we were after the Spear?" asked Nigel.

"I was hired to keep the Spear from falling into Aquarius's hands," answered Sasha.

Nigel had a good idea who hired her but decided not to pursue the matter. "And I'm here because?"

"I think we can help each other," Sasha replied.

"Like a partnership?" said Nigel skeptically.

"I don't like it either. Think of it as an alliance of convenience," said Sasha. "Personally, I couldn't care less about the Spear. I only want Aquarius."

Nigel thought about what she said. While he didn't trust her, he had to admit it was a good idea. "I have to notify my superiors."

"Of course you do," said Sasha as she reached into her pocket and pulled out a cellphone.

"Here's your phone," she said as she handed it to him.

"This partnership is already off to a great start," said Nigel drily as he took the phone. "Mind if I take this outside?"

Sasha opened the door, and he walked outside into a hallway. She closed the door behind him and sat down at the table. She crossed her arms and legs as she waited for him to return. Fifteen minutes later, Nigel walked back into the room.

"Did Daddy say you can play with the bad girl?" asked Sasha with a sarcastic grin.

"Yes, on two conditions, we do this our way, and we get the Spear," said Nigel. "In return, we tell you where to find Aquarius's leader."

She stood up and walked up to him. "I guess we have a deal then," said Sasha as she held out her left hand.

They shook hands in agreement. "Now, what kind of playing did you have in mind?" said Nigel wryly.

"Maybe later," said Sasha with a knowing smile.

"Before we go, I have a question," said Nigel. "Why is Aquarius so important to you?"

"It's personal," said Sasha.

"That's what I'm afraid of," Nigel replied.

Sasha could tell there was no skirting the issue by the look on his face, which meant she would have to dredge up an unpleasant memory. "When I was in Red Curtain, I was sent on a mission to kill him in Dagestan."

"However, there was a…complication that resulted in me losing my right eye," continued Sasha.

"So, this is about revenge?" Nigel observed.

"Not revenge, Justice," said Sasha.

"I don't expect you to understand. The only person who does understand is Simon, and he's gone," said Sasha.

As she said the words, Nigel thought about his time in the S.A.S. and how he spent days being tortured by Siobhan when she was in the

I.R.A. He was reminded of how, upon discovering she was still alive, he had pursued her across the globe with the goal of vengeance.

"Believe me, I understand how you feel, and I can sympathize," said Nigel.

Sasha shrugged in disbelief. "Anyway, what's your plan?"

"There's a group of mercenaries on Sankan that we are going to hire to recover the Spear," Nigel explained.

"I see, and what's this group called?" Sasha asked.

"Monkeywrench," replied Nigel.

"Never heard of them," said Sasha.

Chapter 10
Down Time

Life at the Boom Factory had settled into a dull routine for the members of Monkeywrench. They would each wake up at different times and try to entertain themselves. Since most of the maintenance work was as done as it could be, and most importantly, they had yet to be hired, they sought ways to entertain themselves. Simon and Deon could usually be found in the gym or the makeshift shooting range in the backyard of the mansion. Siobhan spent her days at the soup kitchen with Mai.

When she wasn't there, she was either tending to the various plants on the front lawn of the mansion or reading and exercising, usually in private. While Mack and Dennis either read or watched television. At the moment, Mack and Dennis were sitting in the communications room.

"I am so bored, man," grunted Mack as he reclined on the couch.

Seated next to him at the computer table in a trance-like state was Dennis.

"Don't worry about it, man, it's all good," said Dennis distantly as he looked up at the ceiling, stoned.

"Dude, you need to lay off the weed," said Mack drily. "You're starting to sound like The Dude."

The shooting range was in the backyard overlooking the ocean. It consisted of a table and several man-shaped targets constructed out of wood.

"Be honest with me, Simon, you think this will work?" asked Deon as he reloaded his 9mm Beretta.

"I wouldn't be here if I didn't," said Simon casually as he pulled back the slide on his Jericho.

"You know what I mean, Simon," said Deon as Simon aimed his pistol at one of the targets. "What happens when they find out you and me are still alive?"

Upon hearing the question, Simon lowered his pistol and turned to look at Deon. "I won't lie, I've thought about it."

"And?" asked Deon.

"That's the million-dollar question, isn't it?" answered Simon dismissively before firing several rounds at the target.

*****

Several miles away, in Sankan harbor resided the headquarters of Monkeywrench's only rival on the island: the shipping company known as The Flying Fish Trading Company. However, unknown to everyone on the island, the Flying Fish Trading Company was really a front for the top-secret division of the CIA, Silhouette. Code named Task Force 666 and nicknamed the Goon Squad by Silhouette's director. Their mission on the island was to keep an eye on the Triad and the syndicate and to perform the occasional missions for Silhouette and the CIA. The Goon Squad consisted of two military criminals and was led by a Silhouette agent named Ben Martin.

Martin, a large African American man of considerable muscle, generally wore black pants, a black shirt, and a green jacket with grey aviator sunglasses. The team's sharpshooter was a Japanese American named Kenji Yamada, commonly dressed in a red long-sleeved shirt and black pants with spiky black hair. The final member of the Task Force was a beautiful, short-tempered Cuban-American woman named Fiona Ramos. She had no hair on the right side of her head, while the rest was brushed to the left of her head. She wore a white short-sleeved crop top with blue jean shorts. She was seldom seen without her two Smith and Wesson 645s, nick-named Bart and Lisa.

She kept them in a brown leather double vertical shoulder holster. At the moment, Ben sat in his office talking to the Director of Silhouette, codenamed NARRATOR, on his phone. Seated behind him with her feet on the desk and an impatient, annoyed look on her face was Fiona. Leaning against the wall behind her, chewing gum, was Kenji.

"Very well, Sir," said Ben as he ended the call and returned the phone to his pocket. He turned around to face his team.

"Well, we killin' them or not?" asked Fiona bluntly.

"No, boss's orders," Ben answered.

"The fuck? Why not?" asked Fiona.

"Because NARRATOR thinks we can use them, it might be useful down the line," said Ben.

"Makes sense if you think about it," said Kenji.

"Screw making sense," Fiona grumbled.

"You're just sore because that nun woman knocked you out twice," said Kenji sardonically.

"You wanna die, Ken?" yelled Fiona.

"Not really," replied Kenji in a dry tone.

"No one's dying unless I say so," barked Ben.

Kenji and Fiona stopped speaking and looked at him as he began to speak.

"Our orders regarding Monkeywrench are to observe and report only," said Ben.

"Yeah, yeah, whatever," said Fiona as she stood up and walked out of the room, slamming the door behind her.

"She took that well," said Kenji.

"Least she didn't pull out Bart and Lisa," Ben grunted.

Chapter 11
First Dollar

For the last two nights, Simon, Deon, Mack, and Dennis would gather in the living room and play poker. Siobhan always refused to play, choosing instead to read her Bible on the couch next to the table. The games were fairly recent traditions. They had begun.

"Yo, Siobhan, want to play?" asked Mack as Dennis dealt the cards.

Siobhan looked up from her book. "No, thank you, though," she replied politely in her lyrical Irish accent.

Mack shrugged and looked at the cards in front of him while Siobhan returned to her book.

"How many times are you going to read that thing?" Deon asked.

"Until I find Salvation," replied Siobhan.

"My salvation is right here," said Dennis as he held up a joint.

"Now that's my kind of church," Deon quipped.

They all laughed at the joke while Siobhan smiled subtly.

"Can we play?" asked a female voice with a seductive Russian accent from the hallway behind them.

Siobhan jumped off the couch and pulled out a knife. Simon, Mack, and Deon jumped up and pulled out their pistols. They aimed their weapons at the hallway.

"You picked the wrong house to break into," growled Simon.

"I disagree," said a male voice from the hallway with a suspiciously British accent.

"Show yourselves, or we'll show you the door," yelled Simon as he pulled back the hammer on his pistol. *It can't be him. What would he be doing with her?* He thought.

"When he told me you were alive, I simply had to see it for myself," said the female voice.

Slowly, they heard two sets of footsteps approaching them. As they stepped into the light, they saw that the female voice belonged to a beautiful blonde woman dressed in a black catsuit with a red belt, boots, and a black eye patch over her right eye. Standing next to her was a man with smooth, short black hair wearing a gray blazer, pants, a black tie, and a white shirt. The five members of Monkeywrench recognized them instantly as Sasha and Nigel.

"Sasha," sneered Simon upon seeing her.

"You!" growled Siobhan as she charged at Nigel.

Before he knew it, she had him pinned against the wall. "It's been a while, Devil Woman," said Nigel.

"I told you that's not my name anymore," snarled Siobhan.

"And I told you I don't care," Nigel growled as he pulled out his pistol and put it against her left ear.

He was about to pull back the hammer when he felt a gun suddenly press against his head. He glanced to his side and saw Simon aiming his pistol at him. "I really don't think you want to have a fight with us, Nigel," said Simon calmly.

Nigel lowered the pistol.

"Siobhan, let him go," said Simon.

Siobhan glared at Nigel and released him; she backed away but kept her eyes on him. Simon lowered his pistol.

"What are you two here for?" asked Deon, glaring at Sasha.

Nigel straightened his tie. "You guys busy?" he asked drily.

"Does it look like we are?" Mack asked sarcastically.

"Good, because we need your help," said Nigel.

"With what?" asked Mack.

Sasha and Nigel looked at each other nervously. "Right then, have a seat," said Nigel.

Simon Mack, Dennis, and Deon returned to their chairs while Sasha and Siobhan chose to stand. Nigel stood in front of them like a school teacher addressing students.

"Before we begin, how many of you are familiar with the Aquarius organization?" asked Nigel.

"Who?" Dennis asked.

"Think the Nazi version of Al Qaeda," answered Mack.

"That's one way of putting it," said Nigel drily.

"What about them?" Simon asked.

"A ship of theirs is carrying a certain....artifact to a port in Chile, where it will then be taken to the headquarters of Aquarius," said Nigel. "My government emphatically does not want that ship to reach Chile with the artifact."

"So you want us to storm the ship and get the artifact?" said Deon.

"No shit," Mack grunted.

"The ship is set to depart from Manila in a few hours, so by the time you catch up to it, she should be within range of your helicopter," answered Nigel.

"Doesn't sound too difficult," grunted Deon.

"He's right, it isn't, but I have a question, though," said Simon. "What's so special about this artifact that you would be willing to call us in?"

"Five bucks says it's the queen's sex tape," Mack quipped.

"I'll take some of that action," said Deon.

"Does it really matter? You'll still get paid," Nigel asked.

"We're not risking our lives to get this thing unless we know what it is," said Simon.

Nigel and Simon glared at each other, wondering whose resolve would break first.

"Fine, it's the Spear of Destiny," answered Nigel with a shrug.

"The what?" asked Mack as he handed a five-dollar bill to Deon.

"It's the Spear used to pierce Christ when he was crucified; it's been lost for centuries," Siobhan said.

"So?" asked Deon.

"There's a legend that any army that carries it is invincible," Siobhan answered.

"I'm not one for superstition," said Simon drily.

"Another question, what the hell does she have to do with this?" said Deon, pointing to Sasha.

"Nothing that should concern you," sneered Sasha with a taunting grin.

"Regardless, do you want the job or not?" Nigel answered.

"I think the real question is how much you're willing to pay us to go get it?" said Simon.

"How much do you want?" asked Nigel with a shrug.

"Mr. Faraday, you have the floor," said Simon.

Dennis pulled a calculator out of his pocket and started typing in numbers. "Seeing as how this is our first job and we have exhausted our finances setting all this up."

"Not to mention that you tried to kill one of our people," continued Dennis before pressing enter.

"That should bring our price to… 500,000 dollars, American," said Dennis as he looked up from the calculator.

Nigel gritted his teeth as he heard the number, while Siobhan grinned. "Fine, you'll get the money when we get the Spear."

"Once you have the Spear, contact us, and we'll come pick it up," said Nigel.

"We're going to need details?" said Simon.

Nigel pulled a USB drive out of his chest pocket and handed it to Simon. "Everything you need to know is on there."

"I'll take that," said Dennis as he took the drive before Simon could take it.

"We'll be in touch," said Sasha as she and Nigel began walking toward the front door.

Before closing the door behind her, Sasha turned to look at Simon. "Good luck," she said as she blew a kiss to Simon coquettishly before walking out the door.

"So…just to be clear, we have to keep an ancient artifact from falling into the hands of Nazis. It's like an Indiana Jones movie!" said Mack.

"Who?" Siobhan asked, confused.

"Wait, you've never seen any of the Indiana Jones movies?" said Mack, surprised.

"No, why?" replied Siobhan. They looked at her like she was crazy.

"That's just wrong," said Deon.

"As wrong as that is, we have work to do," said Dennis.

"You're right, Mr. Faraday. Plug the drive in, and let's get to work," said Simon.

"You got it," said Dennis as he sat down in front of the computer.

*****

"Why didn't you mention the Holbrooke?" asked Sasha as she and Nigel walked to their car.

"Because I can coordinate the recovery from there much better, and we believe Aquarius has some naval assets," answered Nigel as he opened the door and got in.

He closed the door and looked up at Sasha. "You know your objective?" he asked.

Sasha opened the back door and pulled out a black duffel bag. "I'm a mercenary, not an idiot," she replied as she slung the bag over her shoulder.

"I didn't ask you if you're an idiot. I asked you if you know what to do," said Nigel.

Sasha shrugged, annoyed at Nigel's tone. "Yes, I know what to do. Just make sure that when this is over, I get what I want."

"I'll make sure of it," said Nigel as he rolled up the window and drove off.

Sasha turned to face the building, then walked away from it to a building across the street from the Boom Factory.

Chapter 12
Smash And Grab

According to the file Nigel had given them, the ship had around fifty armed guards on it, each of them a member of the Aquarius organization. In the cargo hold below was a crate containing the Spear marked SPEERSPITZE, at least according to Nigel. The moonlight danced on the calm sea below them. In the cockpit, flying the helicopter was Deon. Next to him sat Dennis, studying his laptop computer. Simon, Siobhan, and Mack were in the back of the helicopter, checking their weapons. Siobhan was carrying several knives, two M1911 Colt pistols, and an M16 slung over her shoulder.

Simon was carrying his Jericho pistol, wrist blade, and an H&K 416 assault rifle slung over his shoulder. Mack was carrying an FN SCAR and, in his holster, his Tanfoglio T95 Combat pistol.

"Y'know, we really should think of a name for this thing," said Mack as they flew over the Philippine Sea to their target.

"Mack, you are the last person that should name this bird," replied Simon.

"Why?" asked Mack.

"Because you thought Monkeywrench and Boom Factory were good names," answered Simon.

Siobhan laughed quietly at the joke.

"What's so funny?" asked Mack as he looked at Siobhan.

"The better question is why you are wearing that shirt on a mission like this?" said Simon, gesturing to Mack's bright red and green Hawaiian shirt.

"It's my lucky shirt, and besides, you're one to talk about combat gear with that trench coat," answered Mack, gesturing to Simon's dark blue trench coat.

"Touché," replied Simon.

"For that matter, Siobhan, why are you wearing your nun outfit on this mission?" asked Mack.

"For good luck," Siobhan replied with a smile.

"We're here!" yelled Deon in his loud, booming voice that echoed from the cockpit.

Mack, Simon, and Siobhan stood up and checked their weapons for the last time. Deon positioned the helicopter at the bow of the ship and lowered the rear door. Simon, Siobhan, and Mack jumped off the helicopter onto the rear of the ship. Once they were all off the helicopter,

Deon closed the back door and flew away. Deon would fly to a safe distance and land in the water using the helicopter's pontoons and pick them up when they were done.

Simon looked at Mack and Siobhan, who were scanning the area carefully. As the helicopter faded in the distance, a pall of deathly silence fell over the ship's deck. They knew that any minute, guards would come running, drawn to them by the sound of the helicopter like moths drawn to a flame. On the other side of the ship, at the base of the ship's wheelhouse, was a door that led into the bowels of the ship. Simon, Siobhan, and Mack ran across the ship to the wheelhouse at the ship's stern.

There were several shipping crates on the deck of the ship. They were halfway across the deck when Mack saw six guards storm out of the wheelhouse, each of them carrying G36c rifles.

"Assholes at twelve!" yelled Mack as the guards began opening fire.

"Let's introduce ourselves then," said Simon as they jumped behind a shipping crate for cover.

Simon and Mack leaned out from cover and began firing at the guards in short bursts of automatic fire. They managed to kill two of the guards before they jumped behind cover and returned fire.

"Cover me," said Siobhan before any of them could reply. She ran around the crate.

"Any idea where she's going?" said Mack.

"Probably to spread the word of Jesus," said Simon as he leaned out and fired at two of the guards.

Suddenly, Siobhan appeared next to the guards, a knife in one hand and a pistol in the other. She ran up to one of the guards and sliced him across the throat with his knife, killing him. She then punched the next guard in his throat, grabbed him, wrapped her knife arm around his neck, and used him as a human shield. She shot the other two guards with her pistol, then threw the guard to the ground and shot him in the back of his neck. Simon and Mack walked out from behind the crate.

"Thanks for making us feel useful, Siobhan," grunted Mack.

"You're welcome," said Siobhan with her disarming smile.

"What's with the masks?" asked Mack, looking down at the bodies.

Simon and Siobhan looked down at the body of the guards to see what he was talking about. The guards were dressed in black jackets and pants with dark red belts. Under the jacket was a dark yellow buttoned shirt with a black tie. On their arms was a dark red band bearing the logo of Aquarius. On their heads were gray gas masks with red lenses and a black helmet that resembled a German M40 Ns64 combat helmet from World War Two.

"Standard gear of Aquarius foot soldiers," said Simon.

"Freaky," Mack muttered.

Simon gestured to the doorway, "I'm on point. Siobhan, behind me. Mack, you're at the back."

They nodded in agreement and walked into the wheelhouse. They walked slowly and cautiously down a long, dimly lit hallway toward a stairway at the end of the hallway. Just as Simon approached the stairway, a guard grabbed him by his collar, causing him to drop his rifle. Simon brought his left foot down on the guard's right foot, causing him to release him. Simon grabbed the guard and threw him down the stairs. He tumbled down to the bottom of the stairway. Upon reaching the bottom of the stairway, the guard reached into his belt holster to pull out a pistol, but before he could, Simon pulled out his Jericho and shot him twice. As

Simon holstered his pistol, he turned to face the others.

"Can't let you have all the fun," said Simon.

Suddenly, before they could descend the stairway, two guards appeared at the doorway at the other end of the hallway. Mack swung around and fired two shots at their heads, killing them instantly. He turned around to face Siobhan and Simon. "

Shall we?" asked Mack.

The three of them descended the stairway until they reached a doorway at the bottom. Simon opened the door, and they entered a large room with several wooden crates in it and a catwalk suspended from the ceiling.

"Which ones are ours?" Mack asked

"The one that says SPEERSPITZE on it," said Simon.

They walked around the room, trying to find the crate. Suddenly, a guard jumped out from behind one of the crates and tackled Simon to the ground. The guard tried to get on top of him and tried to strangle him with his left hand. Simon flicked his left wrist back, causing the blade to pop out of his armband. He was about to jam the blade into the guard's neck just as the guard saw it and held his arm with his left hand down. Simon took advantage of his distraction and head-butted him as too hard as he could. The blow sent the guard rolling off of him, and the guard jumped to his feet. Simon stood up, still dazed from the head butt, as the guard got closer to him. Simon dodged a punch from the guard and plunged the blade into the guard's neck, killing him.

Before Simon knew what had happened, he was tackled behind a crate by Mack. Before he could ask why, a fusillade of gunfire erupted towards them from the catwalk above. Simon looked up and saw at least twelve soldiers firing at them from the catwalk with submachine guns. Siobhan was taking cover behind a crate in the middle of the room.

"What, no, thank you?" Mack asked sarcastically.

"Thank me for shooting the bastards," said Simon.

Mack leaned out from behind cover and fired at them with his SCAR.

"That'll do," grunted Simon.

Simon pulled out his Jericho and began firing at the guards. Suddenly, five guards ran into the room, heading straight for Siobhan. She swung around to fire at them, but when she pulled the trigger, all she heard was a click. Siobhan threw the rifle at one of the approaching guards, knocking him to the ground. She quickly pulled out her two M1911s and fired at two of them, killing them.

The other three got too close, so she kicked one in the chest with her left leg and hit him in the face with one of the pistols. One of them tried to grab her from behind, but she spun around, slid her gun under his chin, and pulled the trigger. The remaining soldier pulled out his knife to try and stab her while her back was to him. She spun around and hit him in the throat with one of the pistols, then shot him.

The guard she kicked to the floor got up and knocked her to the ground with a shove from behind. She quickly got to her feet and grabbed his face. Then Siobhan swept his feet out from under him with her leg and slammed him down on the hard metal floor. The guard she had thrown the rifle at tried to pull out his pistol. She grabbed her pistols and ran behind one of the crates just as more guards appeared on the catwalk.

"Well, this is going well," quipped Mack. He quickly reloaded his rifle as guards on the catwalk above began shooting at them.

"Got any ideas?" Simon grunted as he reloaded his pistol.

"Why are you asking me? You're the boss," said Mack.

"Doesn't mean I know everything," Simon replied.

"Least you admit it," said Mack with a shrug.

Simon leaned out of cover and fired at two of the men on the catwalk. As he fired, he saw a wooden crate marked SPEERSPITZE on the other side of the hold. "I have a plan," he said as he got back behind cover.

"Damn, and here I was, ready to die," grunted Mack sarcastically.

"Look over there," said Simon as he pointed to the crate.

Mack shrugged and looked where Simon was pointing, immediately noticing the crate.

He got back behind the cover and looked up at Simon.

"So now what?" said Mack.

"Now you cover my ass while I go get the damn thing," said Simon.

Before Mack could say anything, Simon ran out of cover, heading straight for the crate.

"Great plan," muttered Mack as he leaned out from behind the crate and shot at the attacking guards.

Siobhan saw him as she fired at the guards and noticed the crate he was running toward.

She quickly reloaded her pistols and covered him. As Simon ran towards the crate, two guards entered the room and began shooting at him. Simon flicked his wrist back as he approached them. He stabbed one in the stomach and shot the other one. Upon reaching the crate, Siobhan ran toward him.

"How can I help?" said Siobhan.

"We can't get this crate out of here, so we're going to have to open it," grunted Simon.

"I see," said Siobhan nonchalantly as she holstered the pistols. Siobhan grabbed the edges of the lid and pulled on it. After a few seconds of pulling on the lid, it came off.

"Glad you're on our side," said Simon as she casually tossed the lid aside.

Simon looked inside the crate and saw a small metal box; he opened it and saw the Spear. He had no idea why he did it, but he reached into the box and grabbed it. As he touched it, he could swear he heard a voice that he hadn't heard in almost a year, the voice of his late wife, Sheila. He quickly let go of the Spear, closed the box, and picked it up. He walked over to Siobhan and handed it to her, trying not to think about what he had heard.

"Mack, it's time to go!" Simon yelled.

"About time," barked Mack.

They each reloaded their weapons and ran for the door they had come in through. Once they were out of the ship's hold, they ran back up the stairs with several guards in pursuit. Upon reaching the top of the staircase, they ran down the hallway to the exit. As they approached the door at the end of the hallway, a guard suddenly appeared in the doorway. Mack ran at him and jumped at him, kicking him in the stomach before he could fire. The force of the kick sent the guard flying over the ship's railing and into the ocean.

"Way to go, Bruce Lee," said Simon.

"Thanks," said Mack dismissively as he stood up. Simon put his hand up to the communicator in his ear.

"ROUNDABOUT, this is MONOLITH. The parties are over, and we need a pickup," said Simon.

"Roger that. Be there in five," replied Deon over the radio.

"Make it three," Simon retorted.

"No promises," replied Deon.

"Let's get going, pickups in five," said Simon as he picked up the dead guard's gun, an H&K MP5k.

"You're the boss," said Mack.

They ran to the other side of the ship, occasionally turning around to return fire at the pursuing guards. Eventually, they reached the bow of the ship where Deon was supposed to meet them.

"Shit, where is he?" Mack asked.

"There," said Siobhan, pointing upward.

They looked up and saw the helicopter swiftly approaching them. It flew overhead and strafed the attacking Nazis with heavy machine gun fire. The helicopter flew around and landed at the bow of the ship, its rotors still spinning. The rear door lowered, and they ran into the helicopter. Once they were all inside, Deon closed the door and flew away from the ship back to Sankan.

"I just thought of a name for the helicopter," said Simon.

Siobhan, Deon, Dennis, and Mack looked at him.

"The Jolly Roger," said Simon; they all grinned at the name.

"Well, we are pirates technically," said Dennis.

"I like it," said Mack with a thumbs-up.

"Yeah, it's got a good ring to it," Deon replied.

"At least it's not as bad as the Boom Factory," said Siobhan.

Chapter 13
NTBFW

The Valhalla compound consisted of one large three-story building with three Quonset huts on the left and right of it. Draped across the front of the main building was a faded Nazi flag. The compound itself was surrounded by a concrete wall topped with barbed wire. Towards the front of the compound were the training grounds that consisted of obstacle courses and a small shooting range. In the early evening, Friedrich Zacharias liked to walk the grounds of the Valhalla compound and supervise his men doing their daily exercises. In keeping with their Aryan ideals, the men were all white and of German or Austrian ancestry. Many of them were descendants of the original Aquarius forces that fled the dying Third Reich decades ago.

The men, including Zacharias, had undergone extensive military training and were required to be in perfect physical shape. The exercising men were dressed in their underwear as their commanding officer barked orders at them in German. Zacharias walked up to him, a large, burly man with a thin mustache similar to the long-dead Fuhrer. "Guten Tag, Klaus."

The officer immediately turned around and saluted Zacharias with a typical Nazi salute. The men did the same.

Zacharias acknowledged the salute. "Excellent work, Klaus. The men look to be in perfect condition."

"I would accept nothing less. I plan on having them do firearms training later this week," replied Klaus.

"Excellent," said Zacharias. "Carry on."

As he said the words, Zacharias noticed a squad of soldiers in full combat gear sprinting towards the firing range. They were carrying G36cs and Glock pistols in holsters; in keeping with their dogma, they only used German and Austrian weapons. Zacharias was about to walk up to them when, out of the corner of his eye, he noticed Christoph running out of the main building towards him, a frantic look in his eyes and a paper in his hands.

"What is it, Christoph?" asked Zacharias, knowing it was bad news.

"This just came in from Eva," said Christoph as he handed the paper to him.

As Zacharias read the paper, his grip on it tightened. "One of the survivors sent this to us," said Christoph.

"Who are these swine?" hissed Zacharias.

"Apparently, they are some new team of mercenaries called Monkeywrench," began Christoph. "We believe this man with the eye patch is their leader, and this one in the Hawaiian shirt is a Jew from the Guild," said Christoph as he pointed to security camera pictures of Simon and Mack.

Zacharias gripped the paper even tighter as he beckoned Christoph to continue.

"Based on the direction their plane flew upon picking them up, we believe they came from Sankan Island," Christoph continued.

To Christoph's surprise, Zacharias grinned as his grip on the paper lightened. "Sir?" he asked quizzically.

"These Untermensch have made a considerable mistake. But…. their leader is white, so we will try reason first," said Zacharias. "We have an outpost on Sankan, yes?"

"Yes," Christoph answered.

"Good. Send one of our operatives to their headquarters to try reason first," said Zacharias

"Yes, Sir," said Christoph as he turned to run back into the main building.

As soon as he disappeared, Zacharias turned and resumed his inspection of the men.

******

After several hours, Simon, Mack, Dennis, Siobhan, and Deon returned to the mansion. Once Deon landed the helicopter, they disembarked, all of them feeling tired.

"Well, that went well," said Mack as they disembarked from the helicopter, deciding to leave their rifles inside.

"I think we could all use a nap," Simon grunted as they approached the patio.

Suddenly, the outside lights turned on, and they saw a man dressed in black sitting in a swivel chair with a gun on the table next to him. "Do you now?" said the man; he had a thick German accent.

As they got closer to him, they could see that he was dressed in a black suit with a black trilby and black-tea-shade sunglasses with a red armband.

"Who the hell are you?" barked Deon.

The man snorted, "I don't speak to untermensch," said the man arrogantly.

"Want to repeat that motherfucker?" growled Deon as he began to approach him.

Simon held out his hand to keep Deon from attacking him, and reluctantly, he backed down.

"You're with Aquarius, aren't you?" Simon asked.

The man grinned, glad to be addressed by a white person. "Yes, you may call me Agent Scheisskopf," said the man.

Mack stifled a laugh.

"What's so funny?" Dennis whispered as he noticed Mack trying not to laugh.

"Forget it," Mack answered quietly.

"You people stole something from us," said the man.

"What do you mean, you people," said Mack mockingly.

"I'm referring to the Black, the three whites, and the Jew in front of me," answered Scheisskopf condescendingly.

"My name is Mack, you schmuck," said Mack annoyed.

"You're Jewish?" whispered Dennis, surprised.

"Polish Jew…well, my mother was," replied Mack dismissively.

"It doesn't matter. You and the blacks are still Untermensch," said Scheisskopf.

"And yet your boys got their Nazi asses kicked by us anyway," said Mack with a smug grin.

Scheisskopf grunted, insulted at Mack's words, "Why are you here staining our home with your presence?" asked Simon.

"A survivor of your attack on the Eva told us about your brazen attack and that you were flying in the direction of Sankan," answered Scheisskopf.

"How'd you get here so fast?" Simon asked.

"We have a small outpost here on the island," answered Scheisskopf.

"I have been instructed by my superiors to ask you to return the Spear," continued Scheisskopf.

"And if we don't?" asked Mack.

"Then none of you will live to regret it," answered Scheisskopf.

"Really?" replied Simon sarcastically.

"Yes," Scheisskopf answered, starting to get annoyed.

Simon slowly walked up to him. "So let me get this straight, after we just mopped the floor with your guys, you think that you can just walk into our house and insult my friends," said Simon as he gestured to Deon and Mack.

"And that we'd just hand over the Spear, is that right?" continued Simon.

"Yes, I assumed as a fellow white you would have more common sense," Scheisskopf answered nonchalantly.

"I see," said Simon calmly as he shrugged.

Suddenly, Simon kicked the chair, causing it to fall backward.

"What are you doing?" stammered Scheisskopf as he crawled backward.

"Giving you a lesson in who not to fuck with," said Simon as he brought his foot down on Scheisskopf's chest. "See, one of the guys who trained me used to say: NTBFW. Ever heard it?"

Scheisskopf shook his head.

"Thought so," grunted Simon as he pulled out his pistol.

"You see, you Aquarius guys think you're NTBFW. Thing is though… everyone thinks that until they meet someone who really is Not To Be Fucked With," said Simon as he cocked the Jericho.

"And Scheisskopf…you just did," he continued as he aimed the gun at Scheisskopf's head and shot him.

"Good riddance," Deon grunted.

"Amen," replied Mack.

Dennis looked away from them in disgust. Ever since he met Mack, he had been in the presence of death more times than he would have liked, but an act of cold-blooded murder like this repulsed him.

"What's the matter with you?" Mack asked.

"Did you have to shoot him in cold blood?" answered Dennis.

"Dude, he was a fucking Nazi. Besides, how many times have you seen me shoot someone down? Remember what happened in Canada?" Mack replied.

"That was different. They were armed and trying to kill us," argued Dennis as Simon knelt down and looked in Scheisskopf's pocket.

"Simon shot him in cold blood. He wasn't even armed, for god's sake," said Dennis as Simon pulled a small object out of his pocket.

Simon turned and walked over to Dennis. He looked Dennis right in the eye with a look of utmost seriousness on his face. "You picked a hell of a time to grow a conscience, Dennis."

"A word of advice: the next time you decide to start moralizing," said Simon as he grabbed Dennis's hand and held it up to his face.

"Make sure you know all the facts first," said Simon as he placed Scheisskopf's pistol, a Walther PP, in his hand.

Simon turned to face the rest of them. "I think we can all agree that this job is far from over," said Simon. "Deon, you, Mack, and Siobhan are going to check the grounds and make sure he didn't leave any surprises for us."

"What about you and Dennis?" asked Siobhan.

He turned to face Dennis. "We have a shithead to clean up," said Simon as he pointed to Scheisskopf's body.

"What about Nigel?" Deon asked.

"When we're done, I'm going to call him and give him the news," answered Simon.

"Still can't believe you used Nick's NTBFW line," said Deon.

"Yeah. Felt right," Simon shrugged. "Anyway, let's get to work, people."

They all nodded and went about their duties. However, they were unaware that watching them from a small boat not far from the compound was a pair of eyes. The eyes were looking through a pair of binoculars. The man looking through them grimaced, displeased with what he had just seen, and picked up his walkie-talkie.

*****

A half hour later, in the jungles of Argentina, Christoph ran towards the office of Zacharias, a nervous sweat running down his brow. As he approached the office, he could hear the sounds of Beethoven's Fifth Symphony echoing from

Zacharias's office. He knocked on the door, and the music stopped, and he heard Zacharias yell Come in. Christoph shrugged nervously before opening the door. Upon walking in, he gave the customary salute to a superior officer.

Zacharias sat at his desk; he looked up at him and acknowledged him. In response, Christoph lowered his arm. "Well, what is it?" asked Zacharias, annoyed at being bothered.

Christoph cleared his throat. "Sir, the agent we sent to negotiate with, Monkeywrench, Scheisskopf, they killed him."

"I see," said Zacharias dismissively with a lack of surprise that Christoph wasn't expecting. "You cannot argue with race traitors and untermensch."

"Still, they must be punished. We have a ship near there, don't we?" asked Zacharias.

"Yes, Sir, the Odin's Wrath is stationed in Okinawa," replied Christoph.

"The Odin's Wrath…that's the Russian battleship we bought a few years ago, right?" Zacharias said.

"Yes, Sir, we've managed to get mortars for it as well. The ship also has plenty of men and a few helicopters," answered Christoph.

"What kind of helicopters?" asked Zacharias.

"Four MH-6 Little Birds, Sir," Christoph replied.

"Do you want to deploy them, Sir?" asked Christoph nervously.

Zacharias nodded his head and thought for a minute, carefully considering the pros and cons of attacking. He looked up at Christoph, "These people must pay for their attack, send in the Odin's Wrath, and notify our forces on the island to attack the pirates," answered Zacharias.

"Sir, I'm afraid I don't understand," said Christoph.

"I want the Odin's Wrath to shell the island. For too long, the Untermensch on Sankan have interfered with us," Zacharias explained. "It is time we show them all the consequences of involving themselves in our affairs."

"So are we going to war with the Triad and the Syndicate then?" asked Christoph.

"No, think of this as a...police action," Zacharias replied smugly.

"I'll notify them of your orders," replied Christoph obediently.

"Make sure to keep me abreast of the situation," said Zacharias.

"Yes, Sir," said Christoph as he walked out of the office.

As soon as he closed the door behind him, music started emanating from the office behind him.

Chapter 14
Long Distance Runaround

After disposing of Scheisskopfs, Simon told Deon Siobhan and Mack to check the Boom Factory for any bugs or bombs that he may have planted. Dennis was seated at the table behind the computer, while Simon stood behind him, his arms crossed as he watched the television screen above. He heard footsteps approaching from behind him. Simon turned and saw Siobhan, Mack, and Deon entering the room.

"Well?" asked Simon as he turned his head towards them.

"Nothing," Deon said.

"You sure?" asked Simon.

"Yeah, we gave the whole place a look over, and there was nothing or no one," continued Mack.

"Good, have a seat. We're about to call Nigel," said Simon.

"Nice, finally some cash," said Mack as he rubbed his hands together excitedly.

Mack and Deon sat while Siobhan stood behind them.

"Fortunately for us, Nigel included a file on how to contact him," said Dennis as he pressed several keys on the keyboard in front of him. Suddenly, Nigel's face appeared on one of the screens. He looked drowsy and tired.

"Evening, Nigel, rough night?" Simon asked drily.

"It's two in the morning," Nigel grunted as he rubbed his face.

"Thanks for the update," said Mack sarcastically.

"Listen, we have the Spear. When are you going to come get it?" Simon asked.

"Ah, yes, about that," said Nigel.

"This oughta be good," grunted Mack drily.

"Unfortunately, I'm a few days away from you," said Nigel bluntly.

"You serious?" Deon asked.

"I assure you I am very bloody serious, Mr. Bowman," replied Nigel.

"Nigel, Aquarius knows we have it. They sent one of their people here to get it back," said Simon.

"I assume it didn't end well?" Nigel asked.

"Not for him," said Simon.

"I have a feeling these assholes are going to be coming at us with both barrels. What are we supposed to do?" said Deon.

"Survive until he gets here, obviously," replied Siobhan bluntly.

"Much as I hate to admit it, and I really do, she's right," sighed Nigel. "You should be able to take anything Aquarius can throw at you and then some."

"While I'm sure we all appreciate the flattery, Nigel, you realize this is going to cost extra, right?" asked Simon.

"Yes, I'll try to help as much as I can," said Nigel before hanging up.

They were all silent for a minute, thinking about what he said.

"Well, this just went from shitty to shittier," Mack quipped.

"Figured that out all by yourself, did you?" asked Deon sarcastically.

"Enough," said Simon. "Listen, these assholes are not stealing the Spear. We have one week till the Holbrooke gets here. Until they get here, no one leaves the compound."

"That said, Dennis, I want you to call Deng and find out what you can about the Aquarius base on the island," continued Simon.

Simon turned to address Deon, Siobhan, and Mack behind him. "Deon, check the boat and the…Flying Hawaiian, in case we have to bug out," said Simon.

"Knew it would catch on," said Mack smugly with a smile.

"Mack, I want you to go to the armory and find out how much hardware we have left," said Simon.

"What about you and Siobhan?" asked Dennis.

Siobhan looked at Simon curiously.

"I'll help Mack with the inventory. As for Siobhan, guard the Spear and pray," answered Simon.

"It's what I do," said Siobhan with a smile.

*****

At that moment, in his room on the HMS Holbrooke, Nigel sat on the edge of his bed and thought. Best I tell Molotova, thought Nigel. In his hands was his phone, and he shrugged his shoulders and dialed Sasha's number.

For the last several hours, Sasha had been residing in a small, empty building across the street from the Boom Factory. The building was decrepit like most of the structures on Sankan. Conveniently, it was across the street from the Boom Factory. Sasha's room on the top floor consisted of a table, a small chair, and, most importantly, a window overlooking the Boom Factory. Her feet rested on the table, and she leaned back in the chair, asleep.

Suddenly, her phone began to ring; she awoke and pulled it out of her belt. She checked the number and was not surprised to see who it was from. She pressed accept and put the phone to her ear.

"What is it, SABRE?" said Sasha. She listened quietly as Nigel updated her on the status of the Spear and Monkeywrench.

"I see I have an eye on the mansion, no Aquarius agents have been spotted in the area," said Sasha.

"Good, remember your job," said Nigel.

"I will…so long as you remember yours," said Sasha before hanging up.

She disliked taking orders from Nigel, but it was a necessary evil. Sasha returned the phone to her belt, glanced at the duffel bag on the table, and went back to sleep.

Chapter 15
Warning Shots

Morning on Sankan Island came as it did in the rest of the world. However, there was a new addition to the ships docked in Sankan harbor. The transients, Triad, and Syndicate personnel based at the harbor, for the most part, ignored its content to focus on their own problems. One of the few who did pay attention was Ben Martin, leader of the Flying Fish Trading Company. He stood outside their headquarters, staring at the ship, a cup of coffee in his hand.

Alongside him, watching the ship was Kenji Yamada, also watching. "What do you think, boss man?"

"I think I don't like it," said Ben nonchalantly as he took a sip of coffee.

Before Kenji could respond, Fiona walked outside to join them. "What's up, guys?" said Fiona with a yawn as she walked outside to join them.

"New ship in the harbor," answered Ben drily as he took another sip of coffee.

"So?" Fiona asked, unimpressed. "Should I roll out the red fucking carpet for them?"

"If you want," said Ben nonchalantly as he took another sip of coffee.

Fiona looked up at him. "Ya know I have a question for you, Boss."

"Can't wait to hear it," said Ben, his eyes still locked on the ship.

"Do you sleep with those shades on?" said Fiona, pointing to the reflective aviator sunglasses covering his eyes.

"I could ask you the same thing about Bart and Lisa," replied Kenji, smugly referring to her two Smith and Wesson 645s.

"Shut up, Kenji," growled Fiona.

"What if I don't?" asked Kenji.

"Then I'll make you both shut up," barked Ben, tired of the bickering. "Kenji, keep an eye on that ship. I'm going to update NARRATOR about this."

"Why?" Kenji asked.

"Yeah, just another cargo ship," said Fiona.

"I have a bad feeling about it," answered Martin as he turned to walk back inside.

"What do you want me to do?" asked Fiona.

"Keep Kenji company," Ben grunted as he walked inside.

"Lucky me," grunted Kenji sarcastically.

*****

Usually, at this time of day, Siobhan would be at the nearby soup kitchen. However, since the compound was on lockdown, she decided to tend to the garden in the mansion's front yard. As usual, she was dressed in her nun's habit. Her habit consisted of a black dress on top of a white shirt and long gray pants, a black headpiece with a white sash around her chest, with a white collar. She also wore a black head dress with a white stripe on it, around her neck was a golden cross necklace, and she wore brown combat boots as well.

Ordinarily, she didn't carry her .45s casually. However, because the compound could be attacked at any minute, she decided to bring it with her. In her left hand was a small box of gardening tools she had bought from a vendor a few days ago. Upon approaching one of the dead plants, she brushed her long red hair aside and knelt down in front of the plant. Ignoring the hot Pacific sun, she rolled up her sleeves and put on her gloves. She was eager to begin gardening; she started digging up the dead plant so she could plant a fresh seed.

Her digging was interrupted by loud music emanating from the armory. She shrugged, remembering that Simon and Mack would be in there most of the day doing inventory. Deon was at the helipad doing maintenance work on the helicopter, dubbed the Jolly Roger. Dennis was in the computer room researching Aquarius. Siobhan ignored the music as she focused on the plants.

Suddenly, her focus was broken as two jeeps crashed through the gate and drove up to the front of the mansion. Sticking out of the roof of the rear jeep was a soldier manning a mounted Heckler & Koch MG4. As soon as the trucks stopped, four men exited each truck, all of them carrying G36c assault rifles and dressed in the same uniforms as the men on the ship. One of them wasn't wearing a mask; instead, he was wearing a black suit. He was barking orders at the other seven men in German.

Siobhan approached him, assuming he was the leader. As she walked up to him, the soldiers swung around and aimed their weapons at her. She stopped and ignored them. Their leader, the man in the suit, approached her. He studied her with his eyes; he was an ugly man with a rat-like face and a short, thin body.

"Restrain her," said the man in charge.

Obediently, one of the soldiers stepped behind her and handcuffed her hands behind her back. The leader pulled her pistols out of her shoulder holster and tossed them to the ground like they were trash.

"Where is the Spear, woman?" asked the leader in a cruel voice.

Siobhan was silent, staring at him, her face devoid of emotion.

"Ah, I see you won't answer," said the man, his lips pursed in a cruel smile.

Suddenly, he slapped her across the face, knocking off her headdress. Unfazed, she looked back up at him. However, as she stood up, she noticed Simon and Mack walking out of the armory building over the leader's shoulder.

Simon held up five fingers and mouthed the words "Stall them" before disappearing back into the armory with Mack.

Siobhan understood immediately what his plan was. The leader smiled and leaned in close to her until his face was mere inches from hers.

"Do not think that because you are dressed like that and that you are a woman, you are immune from torture," said the leader.

"You are quite beautiful, and I'm sure my men would be willing to take turns...interrogating you," continued the leader as he placed his hand on her cheek.

He slowly moved his hand towards her mouth, a sadistic smile growing across his face.

Ignoring him, Siobhan saw Deon on top of the armory building, holding a sniper rifle, and Simon and Mack opening the door of the armory. When the leader's hand reached her lips, Siobhan suddenly opened her mouth and bit his hand as hard as she could. As he yelped in pain, she jammed her foot down on the foot of the soldier behind her.

She released the leader's hand, and he instinctively, before he or any of the other guards could speak. Siobhan leaned forward and kicked the soldier behind her in the stomach, knocking him backward onto the ground. She then jumped backward onto the body of the man she had kicked, knocking them both onto the ground. Suddenly, one of the Jeeps exploded in a loud fireball, sending the remaining men flying.

"Alright, assholes, let's mambo!" yelled Mack holding an RPG-7 rocket launcher with smoke wafting out of it.

At that moment, across the street from the Boom Factory, Sasha was awakened by the explosion. She quickly looked out the window and saw smoke and flames emanating from the front yard.

"Dammit," Sasha muttered, cursing herself for oversleeping.

Having slept in her combat gear, she didn't need to get dressed. She cocked her C96 and ran outside to assist Monkeywrench.

From the roof, Deon took advantage of the remaining soldier's disorientation and fired three shots in quick succession at the heads of three of the soldiers. Mack tossed the RPG to the ground, pulled out his pistol, and ran outside. He fired several shots at the Nazis hitting several as the rest had taken cover behind the remaining jeep. Following Mack, Simon was firing and hitting another of the soldiers with his Jericho. Siobhan, using a rather painful technique, slid her handcuffs under her legs so they were now in front of her.

She held up her shackled hands. Deon saw her and fired a bullet through the chain connecting the cuffs. Finally free, Siobhan gave a thumbs up to Deon, who responded by giving her a thumbs up. Siobhan noticed the leader and a guard had forgotten about her. She was about to run towards them when she was grabbed from behind by the guard, who she believed was unconscious. He had his arms wrapped around her neck, causing her to gasp for air.

Siobhan started furiously jamming her left elbow into his abdomen. The pummeling caused him to loosen his grip just enough so that

Siobhan could break free. She grabbed his arm and pulled him forward while simultaneously crouching down, causing him to fall on his back. As soon as he was on the ground, Siobhan knelt down and punched him in the throat, thus crushing his trachea and killing him. She grabbed the pistol on his belt, a Glock 9mm, and fired one bullet at the head of the soldier next to the leader.

Then she aimed and fired another shot at the back of the leader's right leg. Siobhan tossed the gun to the ground as Simon and Mack quickly advanced towards her. Siobhan glanced up towards Deon and saw that he had already retreated back inside. She assumed he would soon be joining them in the front yard.

"Once again, Siobhan, good work," said Simon as he holstered his Jericho.

"Thank you," she replied with a friendly smile.

"Not that I disagree, but it would have been nice if you could have left one alive for questioning," said Mack.

"I did. Their leader is still alive, but probably not for much longer," said Siobhan as she pointed to the leader, who was lying on the ground.

Before they could answer, Siobhan walked over to where her pistols and headdress were and picked them up.

The leader was speaking on the phone in German; he tossed the phone aside and weakly pulled a pistol out of his belt holster and cocked it. He aimed it at Siobhan's head as she put her headdress back on. Simon glanced at him and saw him aiming at Siobhan.

"Oh shit!" barked Simon as he pulled out his Jericho. Suddenly a loud gunshot rang out, and the half-dead Nazi soldier fell over dead.

"Nice shot, Simon," Mack said.

"Wasn't me," answered Simon.

They looked over in the direction of the gunshot and saw, standing behind one of the Jeeps, holding a Mauser C96 pistol with smoke wafting from its barrel, was Sasha Molotova.

"Having a bad day?" said Sasha sarcastically.

She approached them just as Deon walked out of the armory towards them.

"You're about to have a worse one, schweinhund," said one of the dying soldiers.

Mack shifted his attention from Sasha to the soldier. He grabbed him, pulled him off the ground by his collar, and pinned him against the car. "Says the dying Nazi fuck."

"I don't talk to Jew trash like you," sneered the man. Mack let him go, pulled out his pistol, and aimed it at his head.

"Fine by me, I don't talk to Nazis pigs either," said Mack.

"This island of degenerates will pay for attacking us, so I die for the dreams of the fatherland," said the soldier, trying to sound proud as he coughed up blood.

"Fine by me," growled Mack.

He was about to pull the trigger when Simon grabbed his hand and stopped him.

"The hell?" Mack asked in protest.

"You can shoot Nazis later. I have a few questions for him first," said Simon.

Mack wrenched his arm out of Simon's grip. "Fine," he grumbled.

Simon shifted his attention to the man. "What do you mean pay?"

The man smiled. "You shall all know Odin's Wrath," he said smugly.

"I see, fine then, Mack, he's yours," said Simon as he backed away from him.

"Thanks," said Mack as he walked up to him and shot him.

"What the hell does Odin's Wrath mean?" Deon said.

"Probably nothing. What I want to know is what the hell you're doing here, Sasha?" said Simon as he turned to face Sasha.

Before she could answer, Dennis ran out of the house toward them excitedly and with a worried look on his face. "Guys, we have a problem!"

"I hadn't noticed," Simon replied dryly.

"He smells like marijuana," muttered Sasha.

"What the hell is she doing here?" Dennis asked upon seeing Sasha.

"Helping us take out the trash," Deon grunted.

"Whatever, we have a serious problem, guys," said Dennis.

"So I keep hearing," Simon grunted sarcastically.

"I'm serious. These guys have a ship in the harbor armed with mortars!" barked Dennis.

"How do you know?" Deon asked.

"I found it by hacking into a spy satellite," answered Dennis.

"I'm sorry, did you say mortars?" asked Mack.

Before Dennis could answer, there was a series of loud booms coming from the harbor. The booms were followed by a shrieking noise from above that got louder and louder. The shrieking was followed by a series of explosions across the city. The bombardment lasted for several minutes. When it was over, several columns of smoke began to rise up all over the island. Suddenly, a loud voice in a German accent began to echo from loudspeakers emanating from the harbor.

"Attention, Untermensch, that was a mere sample of what will happen to you if the Monkeywrench organization does not return what they stole from us," said the voice. "You have 24 hours," continued the voice ominously before cutting out.

"Well…that's not good," said Simon.

Chapter 16
Plan of Attack

The reaction across the island to Aquarius's ultimatum was one of shock and in the offices of the Triad and Vasilev Syndicates, local offices' anger. After being informed by Mai of the number of casualties, Deng called his opposite number in the Vasilev Syndicate. He was an older, corpulent, and balding man who hailed from St. Petersburg, Russia, named Pavel Arbanov.

"I want an explanation now, Deng!" yelled Pavel as soon as he picked up the phone.

Deng ignored his anger. "It's good to know you're okay, Pavel," he replied sarcastically.

"Whatever. It doesn't matter anyway since this is your fault!" barked Pavel.

"How?" Deng yelled, confused and angry at the insinuation.

"If you hadn't convinced us to let those Monkeywrench assholes set up shop here, this would not have happened," said Pavel.

"First of all, Pavel fuck off, and second why don't you calm down so we can come up with a plan because doing this isn't going to solve a damn thing!" yelled Deng as he hung up.

"Deng, is that really the best idea?" Mai asked.

"Wait," said Deng as he held up his hand.

After a minute of waiting, Deng's phone rang. Deng picked up the phone. "Yes?"

"Fine, I assume you have a plan?" said Pavel over the phone in a significantly calmer tone.

"Pavel, you know me better than that. I always have a plan," said Deng smugly.

"Very well, go ahead," said Pavel.

"Glad I have your permission," said Deng. "We pool our resources and attack them."

"That's it?" said Pavel.

"You got a better idea?" Deng replied.

Pavel sighed, "I'm listening."

"We can't attack the ship because then they'd fire another barrage at us, so we attack their office here," continued Deng.

"A good idea, what about Monkeywrench?" asked Pavel.

"I'll handle them. As for Aquarius, they just made the biggest mistake of their lives," Deng answered.

He was silent for a minute. "Fine, contact me with the details," said Pavel before hanging up.

"Pain in the ass," muttered Deng as he dialed a number on his phone.

"So I've heard," said Mai.

"You have no idea," said Deng as he rubbed his temple in exhaustion.

"Deng, what about Simon?" Mai asked.

"Don't worry, I have a plan," said Deng as his phone began to ring.

*****

Pavel Arbanov sat in his office, furious over the day's events. As much as he hated to admit it, Deng was right. Joining forces against Aquarius was their best move. He shrugged his shoulders and dialed the number of his best man. He said, Come in, then hung up. Instantly, a tall man in a gray member's only jacket, long black pants, and black aviator sunglasses with brown shoes and hair entered the room. His name was Orb Marius, a former cop turned enforcer for the Syndicate.

"Have a seat, Orb," said Pavel.

Orb casually removed his glasses, walked to the chair in front of Pavel's desk, and sat down.

"I gather you have an idea as to why you're here, Orb," Pavel asked rhetorically.

"Generally, when you call me in here, it means someone's going to die, so yeah," said Orb drily.

"We've decided to ally ourselves with the Chinese on this since Aquarius attacked both us and them," Pavel explained.

"Of course, why not share the revenge?" said Orb sarcastically.

"Don't be a smart ass, Orb. If I want sarcasm, I'll talk to Deng," said Pavel, annoyed at his flippant remarks.

"Well, the phone is right there," replied Orb drily

Pavel glared at him but decided to let his sarcasm go. "Anyway, Deng is going to call me soon with his plan for our attack on the Aquarius compound, not far from here."

"And?" Orb asked.

"I want you to go with the assault team," Pavel answered.

"Lucky me," said Marius drily.

"Be ready to go when I call you," said Pavel.

"I always am," Orb answered as he put on his sunglasses and stood up.

"Don't be cocky, Orb, these people are ruthless," said Pavel.

"Oh, please, we exterminated these people 72 years ago. These vermin are just stragglers," said Orb as he walked out of the office.

Pavel turned to look out the window behind him, "I hope you're right."

Chapter 17
The Death Game

"It's not that we don't appreciate the help, but I believe I speak for all of us, Sasha, when I ask, what the hell are you doing here," asked Simon.

They stood in the meeting room of the mansion, each of them with their eyes on Sasha. Sasha sat in one of the folding chairs, reclining with her feet on the desk.

"You know, I feel like I did something wrong here?" said Sasha sarcastically. She was dressed in her black catsuit, red belt, shoulder holster, and boots.

"The only thing wrong here is your reputation," Deon growled.

"Why, Deon, whatever do you mean?" replied Sasha coyly.

"Don't play dumb, Sasha. We've known each other too long for that," said Simon impatiently. "For the last time, why are you here?"

"Well, Simon, since it's you asking," purred Sasha seductively in her Russian accent.

"You see, Nigel was afraid that Aquarius would try something like this, so he asked me to stay behind in case something went wrong," said Sasha.

"Lady, shit hasn't just gone wrong. It's FUBAR," Deon grunted.

"What's FUBAR?" asked Dennis.

Before any of them could speak, they heard a knock on the door. Instantly, Simon, Deon, Siobhan, Sasha, and Mack drew their pistols while Dennis instinctively ran behind the couch for cover, expecting a firefight.

"Friends of yours, Sasha?" asked Simon, glancing at Sasha.

"No, I don't know who it is," she answered.

"Right," grunted Deon skeptically.

"Mack, get the door," Simon whispered.

"All we have are pistols. What if it's Aquarius?" asked Mack.

"Since when do Nazis knock? Get the damn door," said Simon.

Mack sighed and carefully approached the door and opened it. To everyone's relief and confusion, they saw Fiona Ramos and Kenji Yamada.

"It looks like we missed the party," said Kenji sardonically, pointing over his shoulder to the burning remains of the Aquarius trucks.

"Trust me, the party hasn't even started yet," replied Mack.

"Good, I like parties," said Fiona with a grin on her face.

"Can we come in?" asked Kenji. Mack looked back at Simon, not knowing what to do. Simon nodded in response, and Mack stood to the side and held the door open for them as they walked in. Fiona and Kenji walked up to Simon as they holstered their weapons. As they approached them, Fiona studied the interior of the building,

"And I thought this place was a shit hole on the outside," said Fiona sardonically.

"Actually, it's a work in progress," said Dennis, standing up from behind the couch.

"So is cancer," Fiona quipped.

"What do you two want?" asked Simon.

Fiona leaned up against the wall and crossed her arms.

"It's a funny story. Actually, we've been hired to fly you all to safety by the Triad," answered Kenji.

"That's not very funny," said Mack.

"Why'd the Triad hire you guys to fly us out of here?" Simon asked.

"Because you assholes fucked everything up in all the right places," grunted Fiona brusquely.

"What my compatriot meant to say is that Deng made a deal with Aquarius to give you up to them to avoid further loss of life among the island's civilian population," answered Kenji.

"And because having the shit bombed out of their island by goddamn Nazis would be bad for business, right?" Deon said.

"Exactly," replied Kenji with a snap of his fingers.

"The plan is to take you and the Spear out there, which will draw Aquarius's men away from us, and they won't attack the city," continued Kenji.

"And with you gone, the Triad and the syndicate can attack the Aquarius base here," Kenji continued.

"You get all that?" Fiona asked smugly.

"As we speak, Ben is prepping the Rum Runner. Once he gets here, we fly you up north into the mountains," continued Kenji.

"How are the mountains any safer?" Dennis asked.

"Well, for starters, there's an abandoned bunker from World War Two up there," answered Kenji.

"Jeez, Nazis, Japanese Bunkers, I feel like I'm in a documentary," muttered Mack.

"So you can hide out in there while Aquarius sends people after you," said Kenji.

"It's really very clever," said Dennis, sounding impressed.

"Bit of a dangerous gambit, no?" Sasha asked rhetorically.

"What's a little danger?" said Kenji smugly with a sly grin.

"So when's Ben going to get here?" asked Simon.

"Whenever he gets here," Fiona grunted.

"And that will be when?" Simon replied.

"7:00 tomorrow morning," answered Kenji.

"I guess we should get some sleep then," Dennis said.

"No shit," Fiona grunted.

"I have a question," Mack said.

"What?" grunted Fiona.

"Are you always this pleasant, or is today an off day?" asked Mack sarcastically.

Chapter 18
Love is a Battlefield

Everyone else was asleep as night fell on Sankan, having spent the rest of the day preparing for tomorrow. The rest of the team was asleep except for Simon; he sat on his bed in his room, thinking as he tossed a ball against the wall. He was dressed in his black shirt and green pants. His trench coat hung on the back of the chair while his pistol and wrist blade were on the table. He kept thinking about that night on the Aquarius ship, specifically when he touched the Spear. He wondered if he was going mad with grief, considering that Sheila had been dead for almost a year.

Simon thought back to those days when they were in Silhouette. While they were members, Simon and Sheila fell in love and married. However, when they were suddenly discharged from the agency, Simon fell into alcoholism. His descent into the bottle cost him his marriage to her. It was only last year when they were recruited by Silhouette to investigate a plot by the secretive organization known as the NETWORC, that their love was rekindled. Simon closed his eyes as the image of her death at the hands of the NETWORC operative, Counselor Black, appeared in his mind's eye.

It was his pursuit of vengeance against the NETWORC that led him to Sankan, his new team, and Mai. His recollections were suddenly interrupted by a loud knocking on his door. He shrugged and stood up to answer the door, glad that his haunting by the past had ended. When he opened the door, he was surprised to see Sasha standing in the doorway.

"Hey," said Sasha casually.

"Yo," Simon grunted.

"Couldn't sleep?" asked Simon drily.

"Dreams keep me awake. May I come in?" asked Sasha.

Simon nodded slightly and stepped backward from the door. She nodded gratefully and walked in.

"It's the fear and anticipation of tomorrow," said Sasha.

While Simon was in Silhouette, he and Sasha worked with and against each other, depending on who she was working for at the time. Over the years, a relationship of mutual respect had blossomed between them. Simon remembered how Deon once called her Simon's reflection in a cracked mirror. She was still dressed in her black catsuit, which accentuated the sensuous yet deadly curves of her body, with red boots and a single cross-draw shoulder holster.

"I know the feeling," said Simon.

Simon and Sasha sat down on the edge of his bed. "Why have you been keeping your distance from me?" she asked.

"Well, for starters, the last time we met, you stuck a syringe in me," answered Simon with a cocky smile.

"Do I look like I have one on me now?" Sasha asked as she held out her arms, a coquettish smile growing on her face.

"Would you be willing to submit to a body search?" asked Simon smoothly.

Sasha brought her arms down around Simon and wrapped them around his neck. She moved closer to him until their faces were mere inches from each other. "Depends on how thorough it is."

"Very," said Simon as their lips drifted together.

Simon knew this was a bad idea, but he didn't care. They both had a strange effect on each other. They embraced each other, overwhelmed with passion. For several minutes, they held each other and kissed lovingly. Simon unzipped the back of her catsuit as he kissed her neck. It fell to her waist, revealing her ample breasts concealed behind a red bra.

Sasha sighed with pleasure as she unbuttoned Simon's shirt until his muscular, hairy chest was revealed. Sasha felt several scars as she rubbed his back. Sasha knew she was the cause of many of them but said nothing. They continued to undress until they were naked. They studied each other's bodies for several seconds before finally giving in to their passion and lying down on the bed.

Their bodies pressed against each other, and Simon looked down at her and kissed her.

The only thing missing was love, but neither of them cared, and they could tell as they looked into each other's eyes. He slid his hand gently down towards her leg, feeling her smooth skin. Gently, he moved his hand up her inner thigh.

"Ah!" said Sasha as her body stiffened with pleasure.

"You certainly haven't lost your touch," purred Sasha.

Simon brought the hand up to her head and rested it on the pillow.

"You did ask for a full body search, right?" Simon asked with a flirtatious grin.

"Mmmhmm," mumbled Sasha playfully.

"These searches can take a while," said Simon as he ran his other hand threw her long blonde hair.

"Good thing we have all night," said Sasha seductively. She gently brought his head to her lips and kissed him. Simon placed his hand in hers, and they made passionate love before ultimately falling asleep.

Chapter 19
Escape into Black

Deon, Mack, Dennis, Siobhan, Sasha, Fiona, and Kenji were at the dock of the mansion. The sun was just starting to rise over the small Pacific island. They had brought with them several weapons and plenty of ammunition. The only one of them that looked fully awake was Siobhan.

"I need some coffee," grunted Mack as he rubbed his eyes.

"We all need some coffee," Deon replied.

"What about you, Siobhan?" asked Mack.

"I'm fine," she answered with her typical smile.

"Where's Simon and Sasha?" Kenji asked.

"Probably spying on each other," grunted Fiona.

As if in answer, Simon and Sasha came walking out of the mansion toward them. "What kept you two?" asked Deon.

Fiona was about to speak when Kenji nudged her in the ribs.

"We overslept," Simon answered drily; before anyone could speak, the dull roar of an airplane engine pierced the sky above them.

pressed a button on it, and the Blues Brothers version of the song Sweet Home Chicago started playing.

"Really? The Blues Brothers?" said Dennis. "We're flying to the ruins of a Japanese bunker to escape from Nazis, and we're listening to the song from Blues Brothers?"

"Yep," Simon replied.

"Pretty crazy, right?" asked Mack.

"Why are you all being so nonchalant about this?" asked Dennis, frustrated.

"Dude, at times like this, it's best to just go with the flow," answered Mack calmly.

"What the fuck does that mean?" Fiona barked.

"See," said Mack as he gestured to Fiona. "That's what someone who can't go with the flow would say."

*****

Watching them take off via binoculars from the roof of the Vasilev Syndicates building was Orb Marius. He pulled out his phone and dialed the number of Pavel Arbanov. The phone rang, and Marius was greeted by a gruff hello from Arbanov.

"Sir, they've left for the north," Marius said.

"Guess our ride's here," observed Dennis as they looked up at the plane.

It was a black Grumman HU-16 Albatross seaplane; the plane came in low overhead before gliding onto the water.

"Ladies and Gentlemen, the Rum Runner," said Kenji, pointing to the plane.

"We gotta get one of those," Mack observed.

"You wish," Fiona replied dismissively.

"Let's go," said Kenji. They each picked up a box of ammo and got into the small motorboat at the edge of the dock.

Once everyone and everything was inside, Kenji drove the boat toward the plane. By the time they arrived at the plane, Ben had opened the side door. Kenji and Fiona got in first, and Deon and Simon picked up the boxes and guns and loaded them into the plane. Once the equipment was loaded, the rest of them got on board. Once everyone was inside, Kenji closed the plane's door and locked it.

"We ready?" Ben yelled from the cockpit.

"Yeah, hit it!" barked Fiona.

Ben started the engine, and the plane roared to life. Slowly, the plane began to move forward. Before long, they were in the air. He pulled a small remote out of his pocket and aimed it at a small stereo on a shelf next to the cockpit. He

"And what about Aquarius?" asked Arbanov.

"One sec," said Marius. He glanced over to the boat in the harbor and raised the binoculars to his eyes. After focusing the binoculars slightly, he saw a flurry of activity on the ship's deck. What most concerned him were the four helicopters being raised onto the deck from the hold.

"Shit," muttered Orb.

"Sir, they have four MH-6 helicopters being readied for pursuit," Marius said.

He heard some indecipherable mumbling in the background between Arbanov and Deng.

"A helicopter is en route to your position to carry out the attack on the Aquarius base," said Arbanov before abruptly hanging up.

"Great," Arbanov muttered as he slid the phone into his pocket.

*****

Several miles away on the HMS Holbrooke, Nigel Solo had just entered the bridge of the British Aircraft Carrier. The Captain, a large, bearded Welshman named Halford, not surprisingly, was already there.

"What's the story, Captain?" Nigel asked.

"Well, frankly, Sir, it seems like the Nazis are planning something with those helicopters," said Captain Halford.

"Helicopters?" Nigel asked curiously.

"Here, have a look at these pictures, a drone took them just five minutes ago," said the Captain as he handed Nigel three photographs.

Nigel studied them, growing nervous but not showing it. Suddenly, a crazy idea occurred to him as he handed the pictures back to the Captain. "Captain, would it be possible for you to hit that ship with a cruise missile strike?"

The Captain looked taken aback by the request. "Yes...but we need authorization for it from London,"

"Captain, we don't have time for this. They're getting ready to go after my people with those choppers," Nigel protested.

"I'm sorry, but I'm not doing anything of the sort until I have authorization from London," said the Captain stubbornly.

"Believe me, I would like nothing more than to blast the bastards back to hell, but I need authorization," said Captain Halford.

Nigel could tell by the look in Halford's eyes that he meant it and that arguing with the man would be fruitless. "Alright then. I'll get you the authorization."

"Excuse me," said Nigel as he turned around and ran back to his room.

Upon reaching his room, he pulled out his cellphone and dialed the number of Felix Proffer, the director of Equinox. After a few rings, Nigel was greeted by Felix's rather gruff hello.

"Sir, we have a problem," Nigel said.

"We always do SABRE. What is it?" asked Felix drowsily.

"To be blunt, Sir, I need authorization from the PM for a cruise missile strike on the Odin's Wrath," said Nigel.

"Is that all?" Felix asked drily.

"Yes, Sir," answered Nigel.

Felix sighed. "Alright, I'll see what I can do, but the PM doesn't like to be woken up at this hour. Even if I do, it'll take a few hours for me to convince him."

"I understand, Sir," said Nigel.

"I'll get right on it," Felix said before he hung up.

Nigel returned the phone to his pocket, feeling defeated. By the time he got the authorization, the helicopters would have already taken off.

Chapter 20
Recycled Evil

"Enough of this!" Fiona yelled.

"I can't take any more of this fucking music," said Fiona as she stood up. Angrily, she walked over to the stereo and turned off the music. She rifled through a pile of CDs next to it until she found one and smiled. She slid the CD into the stereo and selected one of the songs. She raised the volume as high as it would go and pressed play. Instantly, Am I Demon by Danzig began playing.

"Now this is real music!" said Fiona proudly as she walked back to her seat and began headbanging to the music.

"Got any Bon Jovi?" Mack asked.

"Screw Bon Jovi," said Fiona as she began playing an air guitar with her hands.

"The hell's wrong with Bon Jovi?" Mack asked half-seriously.

"I want Heavy Metal, not some asshole from New York whining about his feelings," answered Fiona brusquely.

"Bon Jovi's from New Jersey," said Mack.

"So," said Fiona as she kept headbanging to the music.

Mack and Simon looked at her as if insulted by her words.

"Oh shit," laughed Deon.

"I'm from New Jersey," Mack said drily.

"So am I," said Simon.

"Point proven," Fiona replied drily as she kept headbanging.

Annoyed, Simon and Mack looked at each other, surprised to find out they were both from New Jersey.

"Seriously? What part?" asked Mack.

"Long Branch, you?" Simon replied.

"Seaside Heights," answered Mack.

"Wait a minute, isn't Danzig from New Jersey?" asked Dennis.

Before any of them could reply, the music was interrupted by the intercom.

"Ladies, gentlemen, and metalheads, we're here," said Ben as he carefully brought the plane in for a landing.

"I thought this thing could only land in water?" Dennis asked nervously.

"The Rum Runner has retractable landing gear," answered Kenji.

"Impressive, where'd you get it?" Simon asked.

"Long story," answered Kenji cryptically.

Ben lowered the landing gear, and the plane coasted to a stop on the runway. Upon exiting the plane, they were each greeted by a blast of cold mountain air. Next to the runway was a small, rundown garage with two Jeeps next to it.

"It's like being on another planet," Dennis observed as he looked around at the mountainous, rocky, desolate landscape.

"Naw, it's the same old fucked the fuck up planet it's always been," said Fiona as Simon Mack and Deon unloaded the equipment.

"Elegant as ever," said Kenji drily.

Simon noticed Ben getting back on the plane. "Where are you going?" he asked.

"To refill and reload the Rum Runner, Fiona and Kenji are staying behind to give you a hand," answered Ben.

"Well, that explains her attitude then," Simon grunted.

"Nah, she's always like that," said Ben as he closed the door.

He started the plane and took off once again down the runway. Simon turned around and looked at the others; they had already loaded the equipment onto the jeeps. Fiona, Sasha, Kenji, and Deon were sitting in the lead jeep with Kenji behind the wheel. Mack and Dennis were sitting in the one behind it with Siobhan at the wheel. Simon walked up to the lead car driver's side of the lead car.

"Kenji, where is this bunker exactly?" Dennis asked. Simon, Deon, Sasha, Mack, and Siobhan all stopped and listened.

"The bunker is near the top of Mount Soka," answered Kenji, pointing to the top of the mountain in the distance.

"Great," Simon shrugged.

He turned to walk to the other car and rejoined his compatriots. Once Simon got in the car, Kenji started the engine and drove down a path that led up into the mountains, with the second car following behind.

They drove for over an hour through a road that went up the volcanic Mount Soka. The road stopped near the top of the mountain at a large concrete structure with a large square-shaped hole that the cars could drive through into the mountain.

"Gotta hand it to my ancestors. When they build something, they build it to last," said Kenji as he studied the building.

Farther up the mountain was a large grey cube-shaped structure with a door-shaped hole in the center. Above it, a structure jutting out of the side of the mountain that resembled a saucer broken in half.

They drove through the hole and into the mountain, only to be momentarily engulfed in darkness. Deon switched on the headlights of the Jeep as they kept driving. Eventually, they reached a staircase and stopped right in front of it.

"Everyone, grab a crate, and let's get up there," Simon ordered as they got out of the car.

"Aye, aye, Sir," said Fiona with a sarcastic salute.

Each of them grabbed a crate and began walking up the stairs. At the top of the stairs, they arrived inside the saucer-shaped object at the top of the volcano. They walked into a large room and immediately recognized it as an observation deck. Across from them was a rectangular gap at eye level that ran the length of the wall. Beyond the gap was a view of the mountains, and in the distance sat Sankan City, its malevolent silhouette backlit against the sun.

Once they were all in the room, they put the crates on the ground and gazed outward.

"Hell of a view," said Dennis.

"Yeah, too bad it's a volcano," Mack quipped.

"Wait, this is a volcano?" said Dennis, surprised.

"Yep," grunted Deon as he walked by carrying a crate.

"Great, I feel safer already," muttered Dennis drily.

"Just go with the flow, man," replied Mack.

Chapter 21
Kicking Down Doors

Orb Marius looked at the helicopter window to the mountains in the distance. Beyond the window was the dense forest that separated the city from the mountains. Next to him was the pilot, a Chinese man named Yi Yaozu, one of the top pilots for the Triad.

"We're here," said Yi.

"Got it, Yi," Orb replied before shifting his attention to the inside of the chopper. Inside were six stone-faced hard men, including Orb; three of them were from the Triad, while the other two were Orb's fellow members of the Vasilev Syndicate. The Triad soldiers each carried a Type 95 rifle, grenades, and a Type 92 automatic pistol. Orb and his fellow Russians carried AK-47s and Stechkins. They were all dressed in black, except for Orb, who was wearing his gray member's only jacket.

They cocked their rifles, Orb zipped up his jacket while the others put on their black balaclavas. Orb took a deep breath as the helicopter landed in a clearing. When the helicopter touched the ground, Orb opened the door they all ran out of the chopper. Once they were all out, the helicopter flew away. They landed in a small clearing. Orb, who had been designated as the team leader, pointed forward towards the forest.

The others nodded and followed Marius into the forest. The Aquarius base was located in the middle of the forest, hidden amongst the trees and vegetation. Orb and the soldiers moved silently, communicating only through sign language. As they moved closer and closer to the base, they began to hear voices in German in the distance. Orb held up his fist, signaling for everyone to stop. They knelt and could see the compound through the trees.

The base consisted of two rundown-looking buildings in a clearing. According to the Triad and the syndicate, the larger building was the mess hall, barracks, and base of operations. The smaller building was a garage and an armory. Next to the larger building was a flag pole with the flag of Nazi Germany flying from it. Hanging from the roof of the larger building was a flag with the red, white, and black logo of Aquarius on it. Orb pointed to the three Triad members, then pointed to the garage. They nodded understanding that it was time for them to carry out their part in the operation: planting C4 on the fuel tanks stored behind the garage.

They walked away silently, skulking through the forest and making their way to the garage. Orb looked at the Russians and pointed to the building. They nodded. Orb and the Russians waited while the Triad members planted the charges. At times like this, the mind becomes hyper-aware of its surroundings, the men were ready for anything, their senses primed to attack at the first sign of trouble. The minutes passed slowly and inexorably like years. Orb breathed a sigh of relief when he saw the Triad soldiers returning.

Orb held up his thumb. The Triad members held up theirs and nodded, signaling that everything was ready. The Triad leader, Orb's second in command, held up the detonator, ready to press the button. Orb suddenly held up his hand, signaling for him to stop. Beneath his balaclava, he was confused as to why he had suddenly been ordered to stop. Orb pulled his black sunglasses out of his pocket and put them on.

Both the Russians and the Triads looked at him, annoyed and slightly entertained by the sunglasses. If Orb noticed he didn't care, Orb pointed to the garage and then to the Triad's leader. He made a fist and then opened it. The Triad leader nodded and pressed down on the detonator button. Instantly, the garage exploded in a hellish firestorm that consumed half of the larger building. When the smoke cleared, the garage was gone as well as half of the larger building.

Several Aquarius soldiers, some of whom were on fire, ran screaming in pain out of the building. Upon seeing them, the Triad and syndicate soldiers opened fire on them from the cover of the forest. Each of them fired short bursts of automatic fire at each individual soldier. Orb had no problem admitting that he felt a slight tinge of pleasure at killing the descendants of the people who, decades ago, had devastated his homeland. Some of the Aquarius soldiers who weren't incinerated by fire or killed in the explosion began firing wildly at the forest.

Orb pointed to the compound, signaling to begin the attack. Orb and the unit ran out of the forest, shooting at the remaining Nazis. Soon, the shooting stopped, being replaced by the crackling of fire. The men removed their balaclavas as the Triad leader began barking orders at the men to look for stragglers. Orb noticed that the force of the blast had knocked the flagpole over.

He walked over to the flag and picked it up. He carried it to one of the fires, tossed it into the blaze, and watched it burn. He pulled out his cellphone and dialed the number Pavel Arbanov. After a few buzzes, Pavel answered the phone.

"It's done," Orb grunted.

"Good, any casualties?" asked Pavel.

Orb looked around and was pleased to see that everyone was still alive. "No," he answered.

"Good, the chopper is en route to pick you all up," said Pavel before hanging up.

As Orb returned the phone to his pocket, he heard a noise in the distance. He removed his sunglasses and squinted. He saw what sounded like helicopters flying into the mountains, but he couldn't be sure.

*****

In the basement of the Triads building was, among other things, the Triad's control room. It consisted of several rows of tables with computers manned by technicians while a massive screen was on the wall. In the back of the room was a small office. Pavel walked inside the office and slid his phone into his pocket.

"Well?" Deng asked, sitting at the desk, watching the goings on in the control room.

"It's done, the base is destroyed, and luckily, there were no casualties on our side," said Pavel.

"Good, Aquarius should never have been allowed to last as long as they did on Sankan," said Deng as he poured them both a glass of wine.

"Of that, we agree," Pavel replied as he picked up his glass.

Before the wine could pass their lips, Mai burst into the room, a nervous, horrified look on her face. "Deng, we have a problem!"

"So much for celebrations," Deng said drily.

"Those helicopters on the Aquarius boat have been launched. They're going after Simon and the others," said Mai.

"Just like I planned," Deng replied smugly.

"What?" asked Mai incredulously at his words.

"Don't worry, Mai, Simon can handle himself," said Deng reassuringly.

"I hope you're right," Mai said.

"What does it matter? We got what we wanted," Pavel scoffed smugly as he drank the wine.

Mai gazed at him angrily and approached him, clenching her fist. Before he could react, Mai punched him hard in the face. The suddenness of the blow knocked him to the ground. Before she could say anything, Mai stormed out of the office without saying anything. Deng took a sip of wine as Arbanov stood up.

"She has quite a punch for such a little girl," said Pavel as he rubbed his chin.

"Well, you know what they say: big things do come in small packages," said Deng drily as he took another sip.

"So now what?" Pavel asked as he sat down at the table.

"Now? Now we watch the final round of this little game," said Deng as he gazed at the large wall screen in the control room.

Chapter 22
Dead Man's Party

"I feel like Dr. Evil," grunted Mack.

"What?" asked Dennis.

"You know, Dr. Evil?" said Mack.

Dennis and the others looked at him confusedly.

"The bad guy with the volcano lair from Austin Powers?" Mack continued.

"Oh yeah," said Dennis, suddenly remembering what he was talking about.

Dennis, Simon, Deon, and the others had sequestered themselves in the saucer near the top of the bunker. They were gathered in the bunker's main room, a large empty space. On the far end was a large rectangular slit in the wall that allowed them an excellent vantage point of the mountains. Against the right wall was a ladder that led onto the roof. There was a door on the other side of the room that led to a balcony overlooking a bottomless pit.

Dennis and Mack sat on the floor while Simon, Deon, Kenji, and Sasha scanned the horizon for any signs of an attack. Siobhan sat on one of the crates while Fiona leaned against the wall, a bored look on her face.

"More like Dr. Dipshit," said Fiona bluntly.

"Can I ask you something?" Dennis asked as he stood up, and Fiona shrugged indifferently.

"You've been insulting us ever since yesterday. Why? What have we done to you?" asked Dennis.

"Honestly? I can't stand people like you," Fiona answered. "When I was a kid growing up in the slums of Miami, white-collar assholes like you used to look down on people like me and treat us like shit because we didn't have your fancy cars and suits."

"That's not fair," Dennis said defensively.

"That's another thing. You trick people like me into believing it," said Fiona.

"What?" asked Dennis.

"You say fair like it means something," Fiona replied. "When you grow up on the streets, poor with drunks for parents like me, you learn there's no such thing as fairness and heroes," said Fiona.

"While people like me grew up forced to steal to survive, motherfuckers like you got to grow up in safe little bubbles shielded from the true horrors of this fucked up world," barked Fiona.

"In fact, that's why I can't stand you specifically," said Fiona as she walked toward him. "You don't belong here with your morals and your suit and tie," she said as she put her finger in his face.

"You belong in that safe little bubble you fucking came from, and yet here you are with your holier-than-thou attitude," yelled Fiona in Dennis's face.

"Hell, you'll probably get us killed because you can't even fire that damn thing," said Fiona pointing to the gun in his holster.

So engrossed was Fiona that she didn't notice Siobhan stand up and approach her.

"Go ahead, shoot me," said Fiona tauntingly as she pulled out one of her pistols and aimed it at his head. "Before I shoot you."

As Dennis looked down the barrel of the gun, paralyzed with fear, her words echoed back and forth in his head. Sasha stood by and watched, curious as to how this would play out. Simon, Mack, Kenji, and Deon were about to jump in and stop her when Fiona felt a hand on her shoulder.

"I think that's enough," said a lilting Irish voice behind Fiona. She turned around and looked up into the eyes of Siobhan.

"Killing each other will solve nothing," Siobhan said politely.

Fiona smiled, holstered her pistol, and clenched her gloved fists. "No, but I've been waiting for a rematch with you for a hell of a long time."

"I don't want to fight you," said Siobhan calmly.

"Well, I gotta take my anger out on someone," Fiona barked as she threw a punch at Siobhan's face.

To her surprise, Siobhan caught her fist in her left hand before it could hit her face. "I don't appreciate people threatening my friends," said Siobhan as she squeezed Fiona's hand.

Fiona tried to free herself from Siobhan's steely grip to no avail. Fiona was about to strike Siobhan with her free hand when Siobhan punched Fiona in her nose with her right hand. Fiona staggered backward, dazed from the force and speed of the blow, and fell to the floor. She stood back up and smiled as blood began to trickle from her nose.

"That's all you got? I've fought worse than you," Fiona sneered as she raised her fists.

"I don't want to fight you," said Siobhan calmly.

Fiona was about to charge at Siobhan. Suddenly, a loud gunshot rang out through the room, causing them to stop. Everyone looked at Simon, Jericho in his hand with smoke wafting out of the barrel.

"That's enough," growled Simon. "We don't have to like each other, but we do have to work together, so let's cut the goddamn bullshit!"

Fiona lowered her fists and glared at him, only for Simon to glare right back at her. Suddenly, she laughed before walking away.

Dennis sighed, relieved, and yet he couldn't help but feel like a coward.

"Damn, I was wondering who would win," grunted Kenji.

"Oh shit, get down now!" yelled Deon right before a missile struck the mountain above them, shaking the bunker.

The impact of the strike knocked them all to the ground and caused parts of the ceiling to collapse.

"Fuck was that?" barked Kenji as he stood up and brushed some dust off his shoulder.

"That's some great timing," Simon muttered as he got to his feet.

Mack looked out the window and saw four attack helicopters encircling the mountain. "Shit, that's a lot of a lot of helicopters," said Mack.

MH-6s by the look of them," grunted Deon as he aimed his scoped M14 at one of them.

"Attention, Untermensch, give us the Spear, and you will be allowed to live," said one of the pilots on a megaphone.

"One more missile, and we're finished," said Kenji.

"What do we do?" Dennis asked.

"Just say the word, Simon, and I'll let them have it," said Deon.

"Siobhan, give me the Spear," said Simon, his eye locked on the lead helicopter.

Chapter 23
Burning Sky

"What the fuck?" barked Fiona. "We come all this way, and you're just gonna give them the damn thing."

"Wait for my signal," said Simon.

Siobhan looked at the Spear in her hand and thought about what to do. For then, she looked up at Simon and knew what to do. Siobhan gave Simon the Spear; carefully, he put the Spear in his trenchcoat's breast pocket.

"And what the fuck is that supposed to be?" barked Fiona.

"You'll know it when you see it," said Simon as he approached the ladder. He climbed up the ladder onto the roof of the bunker. He walked to the middle of the roof of the bunker. Once he was in the middle of the roof, he raised his hands in surrender. The leader in the main helicopter smiled in victory as one of the helicopters broke into formation and positioned itself right over him. Inside the bunker, Mack, Sasha, Deon, Siobhan, Kenji, and Fiona had their guns aimed at the helicopters.

"He's gone mental," said Mack.

"I've served with him long enough to know that he's always got a plan," said Deon.

"So what the hell is it?" Kenji asked.

"Don't know?" Deon shrugged.

"Wait a minute," said Mack, glancing at the opened weapons crates. "Where's the Mac 10?"

Back on the roof, Simon continued to hold up his hands as a rope ladder descended from the helicopter above him. Carefully, two soldiers descended the ladder. Upon reaching the roof, the soldiers stood in front of Simon and aimed their HK MP5s at his head. Upon setting foot on the roof, the second soldier walked up to Simon. Both soldiers were dressed in the red and black combat fatigues of Aquarius, complete with the gas mask and helmet.

"The Spear now!" growled the man in front, his gloved hand outstretched.

"Sure," said Simon as he slowly lowered his hands and put his right hand in his coat pocket. Simon wrapped his finger around the trigger of the MAC-10 in his pocket. He reached into his breast pocket with his left hand and flicked his wrist back. Suddenly, Simon pulled his left hand out and stabbed the man in the neck with the wrist blade. Before the other one could react, Simon kicked him in the stomach hard, knocking him to the ground. He pulled the Mac 10 out of his pocket and fired at the helicopter above him. With the pilot dead, the helicopter lurched out of control, drifted to the left, and crashed into one of the mountains.

"I guess that's our cue," Deon observed.

He aimed his rifle at the pilot in the lead helicopter, killing him and sending the helicopter flying out of control before crashing onto the ground. The remaining helicopters responded by swerving from side to side and returning fire. Simon turned to rejoin his compatriots when he was knocked to the ground from behind. He looked up and saw the soldier he had kicked to the ground standing in front of him. Simon jumped to his feet and quickly punched him across his face.

Simon tried to stab him in the neck with his blade, but the man grabbed his right arm. The man punched Simon in the stomach and again in the face with an uppercut. Simon staggered backward as he quickly recovered from the blows. When he looked up, he saw the soldier standing in front of him with his fists raised like a boxer.

"Seriously?" Simon muttered.

The man charged at him. Simon stepped to the side and grabbed the man by the back of his jacket and threw him to the ground. Simon was about to jam the blade into his back. However, the man rolled to the side just as Simon brought the blade down, causing it to hit the concrete floor instead of forcing it back into its casing. The man jumped to his feet and punched Simon in the face with a quick jab. Simon staggered, almost falling due to the impact of the punch.

"What the hell is he doing up there?" Deon asked as he and the others continued shooting at the attacking helicopters.

"I'll go check on him," said Sasha as she ran towards the ladder.

"Fine, Kenji, go cover her," Deon barked.

"Why me?" asked Kenji.

"Because it's the Christian thing to do, now go!" Deon barked.

"I'm not getting paid enough for this shit," muttered Kenji as he followed her to the ladder.

He stopped when he spotted an M72 rocket launcher in the crates. "Couldn't hurt," he muttered and picked it up before climbing up the ladder.

"It is the Christian thing to do," muttered Siobhan drily.

"Not the time, Siobhan," said Deon.

Simon recovered his footing just as the man grabbed him by his neck with both hands. Simon hit the man's ears with both hands, causing him to let go due to the pain. Simon punched him in the stomach and was about to hit him again when the man grabbed him by his collar and threw him across the roof. As Simon got to his feet, the man ran up to him.

Simon braced himself for a punch, but the man stopped and grabbed his right shoulder as blood poured from it. The man turned around to see Sasha aiming her Mauser at him. The man's momentary distraction allowed Simon the chance to attack him. He punched the man repeatedly with his left and right fists ferociously. Simon backed him up against the edge of the roof.

Simon backhanded him and then punched him with an uppercut that sent him over the railing.

"Should've paid attention," said Simon drily; the man fell to his death. He turned to face Sasha, "Thanks, but I had him."

"Yeah, it looked like it," said Sasha sarcastically as she approached him.

Just then, one of the helicopters swung around and flew towards them while firing at them. Simon tackled Sasha to the floor as the helicopter flew overhead, almost hitting them. "I guess we're even," said Simon as they got back up.

As it turned around, they ran towards the ladder, hoping to get back inside before the helicopter resumed firing. Suddenly, the helicopter burst into flames and crashed into the base of the mountain.

"We don't have all day, assholes," yelled Kenji as smoke wafted from the rocket launcher.

"No shit," grunted Simon as they ran towards him. As he climbed down the ladder, Simon pulled out his Jericho and fired at the remaining helicopters while Sasha followed Kenji down. Once they were back inside, Simon climbed down the ladder. Upon getting back inside, Simon grabbed one of the H&K 416 rifles they had brought with them and joined the others in firing at them.

"You alright?" said Mack.

"Could be better," Simon grunted.

"Ditto," answered Deon.

Dennis, Fiona's words still echoing in his head and sick of feeling like a coward, grabbed one of the machine guns and joined them as they continued trying to shoot down the remaining helicopter. Suddenly, they each heard the unmistakable sound of an airplane approaching.

"Don't tell me these assholes have a bomber," moaned Mack.

"It's not theirs," said Kenji.

"It's the mother fucking Rum Runner!" Fiona yelled. The plane appeared in the sky and began firing heavy caliber bullets at the remaining helicopter, ripping it to shreds. The last chopper tumbled into one of the mountains and exploded.

"Yeah, mother fuckers!" yelled Fiona triumphantly as the Rum Runner flew overhead.

"You guys alright?" Ben asked over the radio.

"Now that you're here," said Kenji.

"Finally, some appreciation," said Ben drily. "Guy's, I'm picking up an inbound British helicopter."

Before Kenji could reply, Sasha grabbed the communicator out of his earpiece. "That one for me," said Sasha, speaking into the earpiece.

"Right, I'll meet you at the airfield," replied Ben as he flew away.

"I believe this is yours," said Sasha as she returned the earpiece to Kenji.

"They'll be here any minute," said Simon. "You guys go up to the roof, I'll meet you shortly."

"Suit yourself," grunted Kenji as he climbed up the ladder, followed by the others.

Finally, Simon was the only one in the room. Simon walked over to the balcony and looked down at a deep pit. He thought about whether or not he should do what he was thinking of doing. He pulled the Spear out of his breast pocket. He thought about how he heard Sheila's voice on the ship when he touched it. Another thought occurred to him. If this thing really is as powerful as Siobhan said, then no one should have it.

He could hear the chopper approaching, and he shrugged and knew what the answer was. Simon took a deep breath and tossed it into the lava. He watched as it fell down the seemingly endless pit, then shrugged and climbed up the ladder to join the others.

Chapter 24
Separate Ways

By the time Simon got to the top of the ladder, the helicopter was hovering above them. He recognized it as a Wildcat HMA.2 chopper, commonly used by the British government, among others. A rope ladder descended from it, and a man in a gray suit climbed down it. When he had climbed down it Simon and his Monkeywrench comrades were not surprised to see it was Nigel.

"Long time no see, Nigel," said Simon.

"You know this motherfucker?" Fiona asked, surprised.

"Quite a welcome, isn't it?" asked Nigel rhetorically. "Forgive me for being so forward, but my chopper is low on fuel, so do you have the Spear?"

Everyone looked at Simon, expecting him to hand it over. Simon searched his pockets but shrugged. "You're not going to believe this, but it's gone," said Simon.

"What do you mean it's gone?" asked Nigel incredulously.

"It must've gotten lost in the fight," said Simon. "You could stay and look for it, but like you said, that helicopter is running low on fuel. "Besides, this area is so mountainous and rugged you'd never find it," continued Simon.

Nigel and Simon stared at each other for several seconds. "Is that true, Sasha?"

"Maybe," answered Sasha as she shrugged her shoulders.

Nigel could tell they were lying, but there was nothing he could do about it. He also knew that at least Aquarius hadn't acquired it and that this was far from over. "So, the Spear is gone then?"

"Probably forever," said Simon.

"Either way, we still get paid since you only hired us to steal the Spear from Aquarius," said Dennis.

Nigel shifted his gaze to Dennis and glared at him.

"Crazy how that works, isn't it?" Mack said.

Nigel shrugged, knowing that he was right, not that he would admit it. As soon as he reported the success of the mission to Equinox, Simons' team would be paid by Equinox via their front company, Steed Transports. He turned to Simon and grinned ever so slightly.

"Quite well, Simon, we'll be in touch," Nigel said.

He shifted his gaze to Sasha. "Are you coming, Sasha?" asked Nigel as he turned to climb back up the ladder.

"Yes, this isn't over after all," she said as Nigel began climbing up the ladder.

She turned to face Simon, "Nice to know you can still show a girl a good time," said Sasha coyly. She blew him a kiss as she climbed up the ladder. They watched as the helicopter turned and flew away.

"The hell was that all about?" asked Fiona.

"Hey, look!" yelled Dennis, pointing out to sea, curious that they looked out and saw a rainbow in the sky. "That's weird. It hasn't rained at all."

"Yeah, that is weird," said Simon.

"A rainbow on this godforsaken rock, now I've seen everything," said Fiona.

Chapter 25
Death From Above

Upon returning to the Holbrooke, Sasha and Nigel were escorted to the bridge where Captain Halford was waiting for them. In his hand was a white piece of paper, "Welcome back."

"Nice to be back, Captain," said Nigel drily as they approached him.

Sasha and Nigel noticed that he had a look of confusion on his face. "Who are you really?" asked Halford.

"What do you mean?" Nigel replied.

"After you left, I received a message from the Prime Minister himself ordering a cruise missile strike on the Odin's Wrath," said Halford.

"Better late than never," Nigel grunted.

"My question is, how did you get the PM to authorize this?" asked Halford as he handed the paper containing the message to Nigel. "Why did we spot four helicopters take off for the mountains and never come back?"

Nigel sighed. "I'm sorry, Captain, but the answers to all of those questions are classified. Just know that I'm on the side of the queen and country."

"I see, and her?" asked Halford, pointing to Sasha.

"My own," Sasha growled.

Halford sighed with a shrug, knowing he wouldn't get the answers.

"What about Odin's Wrath?" asked Nigel.

"While you were on your way back here, she departed," Halford replied.

"Are you ready to fire?" asked Nigel.

"I had the missile primed and ready as soon as we received the orders," answered Halford.

"So why didn't you launch them already?" Sasha asked.

"If we launched while she was in the harbor, the blast would have likely killed civilians. We're soldiers, not murderers," answered Halford in a brusque tone.

"What is their current position?" Nigel asked.

"At the moment, they're on a course for Okinawa," the Captain replied.

"Then I guess there's only one thing left to do," Nigel said.

"Yes, I suppose there is," said Halford as he unbuttoned the top buttons of his shirt and pulled out two necklaces with red key cards at the end of them.

"You know what these are?" asked Halford as he held one of the key cards in front of Nigel.

Nigel nodded, took the key card, and followed Halford to a console on the other side of the bridge. The Captain pressed several numbered buttons, and the top of the console slid back, revealing two keyholes, one on the far left of the console and one on the far right.

"It should take one missile to sink them. Do you know how this works?" asked Halford.

Nigel nodded; he referred to the infamous two-man rule governing launches of both nuclear and non-nuclear missiles.

"Good, let's proceed then," Halford said.

Nigel and Halford slid their key cards into each keyhole.

"Turn on three," said Halford. "One…two…three"

Upon hearing the words, Nigel and Halford turned the keys at the same time, automatically launching the missile. There was a slight rumble as a missile took off from the ship, speeding toward Odin's Wrath.

"And that's that," said Halford as they watched the missile disappear into the sky.

Nigel turned to face Halford and handed the key card back to him.

"Not yet," Sasha grunted, her eyes locked on the missile.

"What?" Halford asked, confused as he put the necklaces back on.

"Oh yes. Captain, is that Osprey I asked about earlier ready?" said Nigel.

"Yes, why?" Halford asked.

"Me and the lady need a ride to Tokyo," said Nigel. "There's a plane waiting for us there."

"Right, of course, I'll call the pilot and tell him to prep for the flight," said Halford.

"Thank you, Captain," said Nigel as the two men shook hands. "By the way, we were never here, and this launch was a test firing."

Halford grinned, "What are you talking about? I've never seen you two before, and what test firing?"

"Good answer," Nigel said.

They turned and walked out of the bridge on their way to the flight deck.

Sasha turned her head to face Nigel. "What did you mean back there when you said waiting for us?" she asked.

"Don't play dumb, Sasha, I know where you're going next," said Nigel. "I'm betting that whoever hired you told you where to find Zacharias?"

Sasha nodded, signifying yes.

"I thought so; well, I'm going with you?" Nigel said

"Mind if I ask why?" asked Sasha.

"These bastards killed one of my people, so I intend to settle the score," he answered.

"Fine, but know this: I have no intention of letting you arrest him," said Sasha coldly.

"Good, because I have no intention of arresting him," Nigel replied.

"I'm glad we understand each other, then," she grunted.

*****

Several hundred miles away from the HMS Holbrooke was the Odin's Wrath en route back to its base on Okinawa. In the Captain's quarters, the captain of the vessel was drowning himself in cheap Sake. He was attempting to work up the courage to call Zacharias and tell him that he had failed. He was about to down another shot when he heard a noise approaching outside from up above. Curious, he stood up and stumbled toward the window of his room.

He saw it rocketing toward the ship: a Boeing-manufactured anti-ship Harpoon cruise missile. Before he could act or even think, the missile struck the side of the ship, exploding in a hellish fireball. The fireball swiftly consumed the ship, while the explosion caused water to flood into the hull. Within seconds, the ship had sunk to the bottom of the Pacific Ocean, leaving no survivors. Despite a search by several countries, the vessel would be deemed "Lost at Sea" and ultimately forgotten.

Chapter 26
Final Tally

The Rum Runner landed in the waters not far from the Boom Factory. Upon landing, Ben opened the rear door of the plane and kicked an inflatable boat out into the water. They all piled into the boat and drove a short distance to the mansion's dock. Upon reaching the dock, they all got out and stood on the dock.

"Well, gang, that was so fun. Let's never do it again," said Kenji sarcastically.

"No arguments here," Deon said.

"Damn, and here I thought we were all best friends," said Mack drily.

"Think again," grunted Fiona.

Simon walked up to Ben and held out his hand. "Well, Ben, I can't say it went smoothly, but I will say that we appreciate your help."

"Thanks, just remember, if you need any help in the future, just call and have your wallet ready," said Ben.

"We'll keep that in mind," Simon replied as they shook hands.

Ben turned to face Kenji and Fiona. "Let's go," said Ben as they turned to leave.

As they walked to the boat, Dennis was reminded of what Fiona had said to him. "Wait!" he yelled, the three of them stopped and looked at Dennis, curious as to what he was going to say.

"The fuck you want?" asked Fiona.

Dennis walked up to her, asking himself if what he was about to do was a good idea. Before any of them could react, Dennis turned his right hand into a fist, drew back his arm, and threw a punch at Fiona, hitting her in the nose. The suddenness of the blow knocked her backward.

"Do I belong here now?" Dennis growled, trying to sound as tough as possible.

He turned and walked away from her back to Simon and the others. For a minute, they were all quiet as Fiona wiped some blood off her lip, her eyes never straying from Dennis. The silence was broken as Kenji whistled, impressed at what had transpired.

"Gotta admit, I didn't think he could even throw a punch," said Ben.

"Neither did I," sneered Fiona softly as they followed Kenji into the boat.

"See you guys on the far side," said Ben, glancing back at them as they drove back towards the plane.

Simon, Siobhan, Deon, and Mack turned to look at Dennis, each of them looking either surprised or impressed.

"What?" asked Dennis as he straightened his glasses,

"If this is how every job is going to be, then we are in for a hell of a ride," Mack quipped.

They laughed at the comment and walked back up to the mansion. Simon opened the door, and they walked inside the mansion, eager to go to sleep. As they walked inside, the chair at the computer table spun around seated in it was Deng. "Have any fun?" he said with a wry smile.

"You know I'm really getting tired of people breaking in here," said Simon, sighing.

"I'd recommend getting a better lock," said Mai as she walked out from behind the computers.

"Thanks for the advice, Mai," said Simon, feeling glad to see her.

"What are you two doing here?" Mack asked.

"I just wanted to make sure you all survived," answered Deng. "Plus, Mai was worried sick about you, Simon."

Mai blushed as Deng said the words while Simon grinned.

"It's been quite a day, hasn't it?" asked Deng rhetorically.

"Actually, it's been very boring and quiet," Mack quipped.

"Yeah, I'm thinking of getting a hobby. What about you, Siobhan?" said Deon.

"Just another day on Sankan," replied Siobhan.

"I'm sure," said Deng. "Well, you'll be happy to know that the ship that bombed the island is gone, and by gone, I mean bottom of the ocean gone."

"How?" asked Dennis.

"We don't know the cause, but it was some kind of explosion," answered Deng.

Deon and Simon looked at each other, convinced that it was Nigel's doing.

"What about that Aquarius base?" asked Mack.

"It caught fire and burned down," Deng answered.

"Sounds like an accident," said Mack.

"Well...crazy things can happen in the middle of nowhere," said Deng.

"Like spontaneous combustion?" Mack asked.

"More like explosive combustion," answered Deng as he stood up and walked toward the door with Mai following him.

"Anyway, congratulations on not botching your first job, Monkeywrench. We'll keep in touch," said Deng as he opened the door.

Mai stopped and hugged Simon goodbye. "See you around," she purred.

"You too," Simon replied as she let him go and followed Deng out of the door.

"He's right, this is our first job, and we killed it," said Mack.

"And a couple Nazis," Deon grunted.

"I feel like we should celebrate or something," said Dennis.

"Anyone hungry?" asked Mack.

Chapter 27
A Death Long Coming

VALHALLA, the Aquarius compound, was a large facility in the middle of the dense forests of southern Patagonia in Argentina. It was surrounded by a concrete wall with barbed wire atop it. Inside the wall were two smaller buildings and one larger one. One of the smaller ones was the barracks and mess hall. In front of the buildings was a field used for training, parking, and other such tasks. There was a guard tower on each corner of the compound, which had at least one guard at all times.

The other small buildings were the garage, gym, and armory. The largest of the three structures was the central command hub and private residence of the leader of the entire Aquarius organization, Friedrich Zacharias. The building possessed four floors, with the top one being the residence and office of Zacharias. On the roof of the building was a small MH-6 Little Bird helicopter. The center of the compound was a large field used for training.

At the moment, the compound and the jungle were covered in the blanket of the night, their members asleep in their beds. The only people who were awake were the few guards patrolling the grounds, Zacharias, and a handful of other personnel. Sasha and Nigel silently walked through the jungle, having been parachuted into the jungle via a Lockheed C-130J Hercules. They boarded upon arriving at the Mount Pleasant airbase in the Falklands. Nigel was wearing the dark blue clothes and beanie commonly used for combat by Equinox agents. He also wore special glasses, developed by Equinox's R&D branch, that could toggle between thermal vision and, among other things, display up-to-date satellite info. They were codenamed X-ray specs. In addition to carrying his Walther PPK, Nigel also carried his preferred assault rifle: a C8 carbine with a suppressor and scope.

Sasha was dressed in her black catsuit with a red belt, shoulder holster, and boots. Her long blonde hair was in a ponytail so it wouldn't get in her eyes. Since their weapons came from a British Military Base, Sasha couldn't use her preferred rifle, so she carried an H&K G33 instead. Their plan was to surreptitiously infiltrate the facility, plant several explosive charges on the fuel tanks located behind the garage, kill Zacharias, and then leave on the helicopter. Upon reaching the compound's walls, they stopped and crouched down.

"And here I thought the boys were from Brazil," said Nigel wryly upon seeing the compound.

"What?" Sasha asked, not understanding what he was talking about.

"Forget it," said Nigel, deciding not to explain the joke.

Nigel pulled out a pair of night-vision binoculars. After spending almost half a minute scanning the facility, he lowered them and looked at Sasha.

"Well, there's an armed guard in each of the towers," said Nigel.

"Really? There are guards in the guard towers?" replied Sasha sarcastically.

"Generally yes," Nigel answered flatly. "But I wouldn't worry about them."

"Me and my friends from Colt will take care of them," said Nigel as he cocked his C8.

Sasha grinned at his humor as Nigel lay down on his stomach and aimed his rifle at one of them. He fired at one of the guards, hitting him in the side of the head slightly above the ear. He quickly shifted to the guard in the next tower and fired at him. He did the same to the guards in the remaining towers, the gunshots barely audible due to the suppressor. They waited several seconds in case anyone noticed the bodies.

Upon hearing nothing except for the gentle rustling of the leaves in the trees, they stood up and ran toward the wall. They stopped at the wall and slung their rifles over their shoulders. Nigel pulled a pair of pliers out of his belt and handed them to Sasha. He cupped his hands and bent forward slightly; Sasha put her foot in his hands and climbed onto his shoulders. She quickly cut the barbed wire with the pliers and brushed it aside.

She climbed atop the wall and pulled Nigel up, then they climbed down the other side. They immediately drew their rifles upon landing inside the walls of VALHALLA. Nigel pointed to himself, then to Sasha, and finally to the garage on the other side of the compound. Sasha nodded, understanding that he was going to go plant the charges on the fuel tank behind the garage and cover him. Nigel nodded, stood up, and ran across the compound.

Sasha aimed down the sights of her G33, tracking him as he ran across the compound. Nigel carefully approached the large cylindrical fuel tank. He knelt down behind it and pulled out a tube of plastic explosives. He squeezed it out of the tube and onto the tank quickly. I wish Stapleton could have seen this thought, Nigel, as he squeezed the white putty out of the tube.

Once all the plastic explosives were on the tank, he stuck a remote detonator in the substance that would allow him to set off the explosion from a distance with a trigger. Satisfied with his job, he stood up and peeked around the corner, looking directly at where Sasha was hiding. He pulled a flashlight the size of a pen out of his pocket and flashed it at Sasha twice. Sasha saw Nigel's light flashing, signaling that the charges were planted and that they were ready to storm the command center. She pulled out a flashlight of her own and flashed it at him, indicating that she understood.

She stood up and ran towards the front door of the command center. Nigel stood on the left side of the door, while Sasha stood on the right side. They looked at each other and nodded, silently saying that they were ready. They took a deep breath and kicked open the door.

As they ran inside, they scanned the corners with their guns instinctively. The room was medium-sized, with electronic equipment and furniture strewn about. Suddenly, they heard footsteps descending a staircase on the other side of the room. Upon reaching the bottom of the staircase, Christoph immediately saw Nigel and Sasha. Before any of them could react, he reached for his pistol and started shooting at them.

Nigel and Sasha ducked behind a table while Christoph began retreating up the staircase. Sasha stood up from behind the table and fired a short burst at him, hitting him in the head. Before they could say or do anything, an alarm sounded.

"So much for subtlety," said Nigel as the alarm blared overhead.

"Subtlety is overrated," Sasha grunted.

"We need to move before Zacharias gets onto that helicopter," said Nigel.

"Then let's move," barked Sasha as she ran up the staircase with Nigel following behind her.

Luckily, Christoph was the only person in the building except for Zacharias. As they reached the second floor, Nigel pulled out the detonator for the charges. Sasha noticed him turn it on.

"Let's give them something to worry about besides us," said Nigel as he pressed the trigger. Immediately, the tank exploded in a hellish fireball.

"That should keep the bastards busy," Nigel quipped.

"Not for long," said Sasha as she turned toward the staircase.

Nigel followed Sasha up the stairs to the third floor and to the fourth. Upon reaching the fourth floor, they could hear the helicopter engine starting.

"Bloody hell," muttered Nigel as they followed the sound up the stairs to the roof.

As they reached the roof, they saw Zacharias running toward the helicopter. Nigel shot first, hitting the pilot and grounding them. Zacharias swung around, enraged. He pulled out a Luger pistol and fired several shots at Nigel. His first shot missed, but one of the bullets hit him in the shoulder, knocking him to the ground. Before Zacharias could fire another shot, Sasha raised her rifle and shot him in the left leg.

He fell to the floor with a cry like a wounded animal as blood poured from his wound. Sasha casually tossed her rifle to the ground and walked over to him. He looked up from his wound and saw her approaching him. He quickly reached for his Luger as Sasha pulled out her Mauser. Just as he was about to grab it, she crushed his hand with her foot.

As Zacharias held his injured hand, he looked up at her and recognized her, to his surprise. "You…the woman from my dream."

"I'm glad you still remember what you did in Dagestan," said Sasha as she cocked the pistol and aimed it at his forehead.

Zacharias grinned as if complimented, "How's the eye? You Russian bi..." said Zacharias.

Before he could finish speaking, Sasha pulled the trigger, killing him. "It's better now," she said coldly.

She turned to face Nigel. He was sitting on the floor, putting pressure on his bullet wound to stop the bleeding.

She walked over to him and knelt down. "Are you alright?" asked Sasha.

"Fine, I've been shot before," answered Nigel.

Sasha knelt down and gave his wound as quick a field dressing as she could. "That'll do for now. We need to leave," she said as she helped him up.

Nigel leaned on her shoulder as they walked to the helicopter. Sasha opened the right door and helped Nigel in, then ran to the other side. She pulled the body of the pilot out and tossed it onto the roof. Finally, she got inside and closed the door. As she was getting ready to take off, three armed Aquarius soldiers burst through the door onto the roof. Nigel quickly pulled out his

PPK and fired three shots at their heads before they could raise their guns.

He looked at Sasha. "Can't let you have all the fun," said Nigel weakly as the helicopter began to rise in the air.

Sasha smiled at the humor as she flew the helicopter away from the compound.

Nigel looked back at the compound and saw the fire spreading to the other buildings. "Paybacks a bitch, isn't it?"

"Yes, considerably," replied Sasha.

"Mind if I ask you a question?" asked Nigel as he looked away from the compound to Sasha.

"Depends on the question," Sasha grunted.

"Why?" asked Nigel.

"Why did you want him dead and don't say because he was a Nazi," asked Nigel.

She looked at him and pointed to her eye patch. "This is why,"

"I thought it was because of Simon," said Nigel jokingly.

Sasha smiled at the memory of her night with Simon but said nothing. "Is that what the file you have on me says?" she asked.

"I don't know what you're talking about," said Nigel dismissively with a slight grin.

Sasha smiled at the answer.

Chapter 28
From on High

Sasha and Nigel parted ways in Buenos Aires just like they had planned. She had returned to her Villa on the Spanish coast. As her taxi pulled up to her villa, she noticed a black car parked outside. She was wearing her red shirt, black jacket, pants, and red boots. She retrieved her small traveling bag, containing her catsuit and equipment, and paid the driver. As soon as he left, she opened her bag and pulled out her Mauser.

She walked up to the door and cocked the pistol. She took a deep breath, kicked it open, and ran inside. Instead of being greeted with gunfire, she saw two men seated at her kitchen table drinking tea. They were both dressed in black pea coats, pants, and sunglasses with gloves and a white shirt with a clerical collar. Their black hair was smoothed back. Sasha knew who they were the minute she saw them. On the table was a large metal briefcase. Casually, the two men looked at her and stood up.

"You have a lovely home, Miss Molotova," said one of the men as they approached her.

"I wasn't aware I would be entertaining the Vatican," Sasha said sarcastically.

"I am Father Paulo," said the man.

"This is Father Carlos," said Father Paulo as he gestured to the other man. "Please lower your gun. We mean you no harm."

"Toss yours on the floor first," said Sasha.

The two men looked at each other and back at her. "Very well," said Father Paulo.

They reached into their jackets, pulled out their pistols, and dropped them on the floor. Sasha kicked them to the side and lowered her Mauser.

"I know who you two are, your Disciple 13," said Sasha.

"Then you know why we're here?" said Father Paulo.

"Do you have it?" Father Carlos asked.

"No, it was lost in the fighting," Sasha answered.

"That is…regrettable, but it is better no one have it than for the enemies of his holiness," said Father Paulo.

"What about Aquarius?" asked Father Carlos.

"The Intel you gave me on his location was accurate. Zacharias is dead," Sasha answered.

"Good, Carlos, give her the money," said Father Paulo.

Father Carlos handed her the briefcase, and she took it and opened it. Inside was several million dollars. She closed it and looked up at them.

"I get why you wanted the Spear, but why did you want Zacharias dead and VALHALLA destroyed?" Sasha asked.

"We received word that there were certain… "Controversial" documents from the war that we could not risk getting out," answered Father Paulo.

Sasha smirked, not surprised. "Thanks to you, the Holy See's reputation remains untarnished," Father Paulo continued.

"Right now, get out," said Sasha.

The two men picked up their guns and walked to the door. "We'll be in touch," said Father Carlos as they walked out the door.

Sasha walked over to the couch; she tossed the suitcase and her bag to the ground and sat down exhausted. She looked out the window at the Alboran Sea and smiled.

"I need a vacation," Sasha muttered.

*****

In the days since their battle with Aquarius, the members of Monkeywrench had resumed their daily routines while awaiting another job. Simon sat in the back patio, looking out at the sea, thinking about that incident on the ship with the Spear. So lost in thought was he that he didn't hear Deon approaching him.

"Hey man, what's up?" Deon asked.

Simon turned around to face Deon. "Nothing, really."

"Y'know, I was thinking about the Spear," said Deon. "Specifically about what happened to it,"

"It is a mystery," said Simon dismissively.

"Come on, Simon, you know what I'm getting at," said Deon. "What did you do with the Spear of Destiny?"

"I threw it in the volcano," Simon answered bluntly,

"Okay....why? The damn things priceless?" asked Deon.

"You wouldn't believe me if I told you," Simon said.

"Dude, after all the shit you and I saw in Silhouette, try me," said Deon.

Simon sighed. "When we were on the ship, and I touched the Spear, I swear I heard Sheila call my name."

Deon was quiet for a minute as he let the enormity of what Simon said sink in. "Seriously?"

"Yeah, it was like destroying it was the right thing to do," said Simon.

Deon took one look at Simon and knew he wasn't joking. "That's like some Indiana Jones type shit,"

"Tell me about it, I half expected to hear the theme song start playing," Simon replied.

Deon grinned at Simon, sarcasm, "Maybe Siobhan was right, and the Spear is magic or something."

"If it was her, do you think she was trying to tell you something?" said Deon.

"Like what?" Simon asked.

"Maybe it was her way of telling you that she's okay," said Deon.

Simon thought about Deon's words. It was a comforting thought that he hoped was true. "Who knows, either way, I still miss her though."

"So do I, man, she was the best," said Deon.

"Damn right," Simon agreed.

Deon turned to walk back inside, and Simon was about to follow him. He turned around and looked out at the sea; the sun was shining on the clear blue waters of the Devil's Sea. He looked up at the sky and didn't see a single cloud. Simon smiled, positive that Sheila was in a better place. He still didn't know what he had heard on that ship, but it felt good hearing Sheila's voice again. Either way, Simon had a feeling that Sheila was telling him it was time for him to move on.

Simon looked up at the sky and grinned. "Save a place for me, hon," said Simon softly.

He turned and rejoined his teammates inside the Boom Factory.

About the Author

Robert Fisher was born in Long Branch, New Jersey. While attending Indian River State College in Florida, he began writing as a hobby that quickly turned into a passion for storytelling. After graduating from college, he sought to have his work published. He can be contacted on Facebook and Twitter at @ShadowWorld19. Live to Die Twice is his eighth book. If you enjoyed it, get ready because the best is yet to come.....

The secrets of the past, present, and future are revealed in book nine of the Shadow World saga: The Shadow World Files...

Other Books by Robert Fisher

Sanction Blue
Edge Of The Abyss
Hell To Pay
Death Dealers Incorporated
No One Lives Forever
Never Say Forever
Vengeance Is Forever